D1412369

Ding Ding

written by:

EDDIE JOE BUSH

iUniverse, Inc.
New York   Bloomington

Ding Ding

This is a work of fiction. All of the characters, names, incidents, organizations, and dialogue in this novel are either the products of the author's imagination or are used fictitiously.

iUniverse books may be ordered through booksellers or by contacting:

iUniverse
1663 Liberty Drive
Bloomington, IN 47403
www.iuniverse.com
1-800-Authors (1-800-288-4677)

Because of the dynamic nature of the Internet, any Web addresses or links contained in this book may have changed since publication and may no longer be valid. The views expressed in this work are solely those of the author and do not necessarily reflect the views of the publisher, and the publisher hereby disclaims any responsibility for them.

ISBN: 978-0-595-52414-3(pbk)
ISBN: 978-0-595-62468-3 (ebk)

Printed in the United States of America

Chapter One

For the most part of his life Albert Wise had been in and out of yougth authortiy facilities and jails for assault and battery, robbery, and carrying a firearm without a license. He dropped out of high school during the first semester of his freshman year. But had managed to get his G.E.D. when he was in Lompoc for stealing mail off of a vacant mail truck. Someone saw it and followed him from a distance on foot then called the police and told them where they'd seen him stash the mailbag. It was a federal crime. So the idea he had of cashing any checks the hidden sack had in it went sour when the F.B.I. busted him.

In prison his ability to read and spell improved a great deal as the consequence of learning to use a dictionary and becoming an avid reader of mystery books. After about three years he got out. And discovered that his seemingly meaningless job inside the place as a janitor helped him to land an entry level janitorial position working at the local community emergency clinic, with a good word from one of his ex-probation officers. He quickly made friends with old man Cody, the night security guard there. And his respect for the old timer and the wise advice that he always got from him helped to keep Al on the right track. A womanizer instead of a criminal. And he became as devoted to building a reputation as a lover-boy, as he was to reading a dam good mystery book whenever he ran across one.

During that time Al was around the age of twenty-five. And after he'd gotten out of the big house had crawled in and out of a many young girls bedroom windows in the wee hours of the night and early morning.

Sometimes with a very narrow escape. Like the time when Margaret's father tapped on her bedroom door and he had to skeet out of the window butt naked and over the brick fence not to get caught with her. The neighbor's backyard was the only place he had to go not to be seen by someone outside without any clothes on. Just luckily the vicious dog that the neighbors had was tied up and nobody in the house cared to bother with going outside to investigate the reason why it suddenly started barking and snarling so loud. When the coast was clear it was real funny to Margaret watching Al creep back to her window with his hands covering his private parts. So, for a long time Al wouldn't even mention that girl's name. He hated her. Because laughing about his helpless situation that night hadn't been enough for her. No. She had to add insult to injury, by using the power she had to either give or not give him his clothes back, to force him to make a complete fool of himself hopping around like a bunny rabbit flapping his arms like a seagull. Or else, walk home naked. Don't get me wrong now. He had a bizarre sense of humor himself and was pretty good at telling some weird jokes. A skill that he acquired from spending so much time around criminals. But he felt like, no man ought to be clowned by a woman the way Margaret did him that night.

There was one window, however, that he always wanted to crawl into but never could. Linda Smith's. Linda was the kind of girl that made good grades in high school, was attending college, and cooked and cleaned house to earn an allowance from her parents. Who both worked and were buying a home in the middle-class neighborhood that was near the clinic where Al was a janitor. Their house sat across the street from 109th Street Park. The place where Al often went to hang out. And so did Linda.

When they were both younger every so often a disc jockey named Monteque would sponsor a dance party at the park in the gymnasium. Which is how Al eventually met Linda. They were at one of Monteque's oldie but goodie partys one night and accidently bumped into each other doing the cha cha while "Hello Stranger" by Barbara Mason was playing. Immediately Al noticed that she had plain but elegant facial features. But that body Linda had to go with it made her as fine as a bottle of rare wine. After that he kept his eye on her. And mingled close by waiting for an opportunity to pick her for a slow dance with. And when the D.J.

put "O-o-o-h Baby, Baby" by Smokey Robinson on his turntable, that was it. He grabbed her before anybody else had the chance to. They embraced and leaned into each other and began moving in rhythmic sways, turns, and steps. Ever so discretely, doing a little bumping and grinding. When the record was over they took time to sit out a few dances so they could talk and get acquainted. And when the dance party was over, even though Linda didn't leave with him, he had her telephone number in his pocket. But he got locked up and never did any more than cum in his pants that dance night.

On this particular day it was years later, on a breezy Sunday morning in the summer when Al came out of Sam's Liquor Store with a bottle of cheap but good tasting wine and several cups in a brown paper bag. Sam's was another one of the local hangouts, besides 109th Street Park, where a lot of petty hustlers and want-to-be gangsters rendezvoused to shoot dice, get high in any number of different ways, and peddle off some type of illicit merchandise on the side of the liquor store near the alley in back of it. But that day the usual crowd of thugs weren't hanging around at Sam's, probably because it was too early, and actually, just too nice of a day. So after Al left the liquor store he headed over to the park.

His intentions were for him and his pit bull Butch, who was tagging along, to settle down at the table under the old elm tree that sat on the far side of the playground near the horseshoe pit. But as he walked through the park gate, saw that someone else had beaten him to the secluded spot. It was a woman. She was smiling watching him approach. And when he got close enough, saw that it was Linda. Then he began smiling. Thinking that it just might be his lucky day.

As soon as she saw the man and dog come through the open gate she knew it was Al. And that she was about to have some fun listening to him invent the most ingenious things to say that he believed would persuade her to let him get between her legs. That, and the way he walked, with a sort of bop, were the things that had never changed about him from the time they first met each other. It wasn't that Linda didn't think that Al was good in bed, as a matter of fact, she knew he was from the reputation that he had. But just the same, Al wasn't her type. He knew that too inside his heart. Nevertheless, the challenge that Linda presented always brought out the best mack that he could think of. And although what he told Linda never worked on her, it did on other girls. When Al reached the table Linda slid over to make room for him. As Butch got situated beneath the part of the bench that she had her feet on. The tree branches of the elm hung low and supplied them with plenty of shade.

As usual, Al didn't waste any time spitting flatter out of his mouth. Which Linda knew always preluded to Al hitting on her for some pussy. But she finessed her way out of that situation this time by asking him to tell her something funny. By then Al had the bottle of wine sitting between Linda and himself and was holding a cup of it, that he sat down, after she abruptly interrupted his folly. And with a quizzical expression and tone of voice he responded by posing what she had just asked him to do as a question to her. "Tell you something funny?" That prompted him to reach into his pants pocket and pull out a drawstring tobacco pouch that had some marijuana and cigarette rolling papers inside. Linda watched him sprinkle a small amount of the weed into the folded center of a Zig Zag then roll the paper back and forth using his fingertips to evenly spread the substance and form it into a stick. And then, slide the tip of his tongue along the dried gluey edge of the paper to hold the joint together. Al lit it and drew the smoke deep inside his lungs. And said to Linda as he held his breath, "Why don't you take a hit on this joint and a sip of this good tasting wine? That'll make you laugh." Then he exhaled, hardly blowing out any smoke at all.

"I'm sure it would. But I don't get high."

"Well, now that I think about it, what you seem to really be asking me to do is entertain you."

"Yes. That would be nice for a change. Don't you think?"

"So, what do you want to hear? Some silly stuff that I remember that happened to people when I was locked up?"

"How 'bout a story? Tell me one that you've read about."

Al took a look to see the state of disposition that Butch was in before he answered Linda. And saw that he himself was being entertained by the basketball game that was going on in the distance. Once he was satisfied that his dog was OK he adjusted himself back into his sitting position on top of the park table and mumbled, "A story huh." And with more clarity said, "Well, let me think... Have you heard the one called 'Ding Ding'?"

"No."

"Alright. There was this married couple, who'd about twice a week, walk past this retarded school. A young boy by the name of Ken went there about the age of 11 or 12. By coincidence, nearly every time the couple passed by, the boy would be hanging around the school's fence that was only a foot or two from the sidewalk. Eventually the couple and boy made friends with each other. And just between themselves, the man and his wife nicknamed the boy Ding Ding. But never called him that to his face. Giving Ken that nickname wasn't a sick joke the couple was playing on the poor kid, but instead, what they had started calling him because they noticed that he would say that to them whenever the school bell rung signaling the end of his recess period. Their relationship with the boy went on for a long while without them ever suspecting that Ken lived in the same neighborhood as they did, and that, after he was trained to do certain things for himself he would be graduating from the school. When he did, the couple had no idea why they didn't see him anymore. And didn't find that out, until, one day, Ken was riding in the car with his mother and she happened to drive down the street that the man and his wife lived on and he spotted them walking home. He started yelling, "Them my friends! Stop! Them my friends Momma!" And made a ruckus that was so bad his mother had no choice but to slow down, pull over, and park the car. It happened so close to the couple that they couldn't help but notice that whoever the woman was in the car, she was having a big problem controlling her kid. When she got out of the car, to their amazement, she started across the street walking towards them holding Ding Ding by the hand. The man and his wife admitted that they knew her son. And since they were, by then, right at their doorstep, invited Ken and his mother to come in for a while. After they got acquainted the boy's mother thought it to be a good idea to leave her phone number with the couple, just in case either one of them ever saw her retarded son wondering around by himself somewhere. Well, one day it happened to the husband of the couple when he went outside to collect his newspaper off the front porch. By some miracle the boy had made it back to where he lived, and was pulling a little red toy wagon into his driveway on the side of his house. After talking to Ken for a moment or two the man was able to find out that he'd come there wanting to visit again. He tried to explain to the boy as nice as he could that it wasn't a good time for that because he had to get ready to go to work. Normally his wife would have been there to help out but wasn't because she'd gotten caught up in a traffic jam. So as soon as the man got the boy inside he called his mother to come over and pick him up. But her problem was, her car was in the repair shop and she'd have to walk. So it was going to take much longer for her to get there. Because of that and knowing that a five or six minute drive amounted to a thirty-five to forty-five minute walk the man decided that he had no choice but to lead Ken into the kitchen with him so he could keep the boy company while he made his lunch. Unfortunately, when he did that the boy spotted the cookies that he was packing for desert. And he wanted some. Suddenly, it occurred to the man that giving Ding Ding something to eat would be a good way to keep him occupied while he took his shower. So he dug out a t.v. dinner tray and closed the lid on the toilet seat in his bathroom, had Ken sit there, and gave him a can of soda pop to go with the cookies because he was out of milk from breakfast. Satisfied that he had the boy under his control the man disrobed inside of the shower with the curtain pulled closed and began to bathe. At first the man peeped out to check on Ken every few seconds. Then did it less and less, until, he felt comfortable that he could go ahead and finish bathing without checking on the boy again until he was through. Which was a bad decision on his part. Because what he had given Ken to eat he was allergic to. And slowly he became dude that made the movie Chiller and wanted to get his freak on. At first the man thought it was his wife who was pulling back the shower curtain, thinking that she had finally made it home. But when he called her name and got no answer, he opened his eyes and discovered Ding Ding had pulled the curtain back and was climbing into the tub with a rock-hard on. And for the boy's age he had a big one too. As soon as the man realized that he began to struggle with the boy to keep him out.

The man found himself being overpowered and the shock of it made his knees go weak, causing him to slide down the boy's body with the side of his face dragging against his chest and stomach. And it was only because the boy was older and stronger than when the man and his wife first met him that he was able to bare the weight of the man's grip around his legs. And you know when scared people get a hold on you they harder to shake loose than a crawfish is got you by the lip! They eyes be bucked and tongue hanging out. So, naturally, the man was pleading for his life with slobber coming from his mouth as he lowered his head down begging for mercy. In the process, the boy's thing went into the man's mouth. Then all he could think to do was suck on it hoping that would stop the boy's attack on him and save his life. While that was going on in the bathroom, the man's wife and boy's mother arrived at the house at the same time and walked in together. After they exchanged greetings Ken's mother began to explain why she had come there. As that was happening in the living room back in the bathroom, and unbeknown to the women, the man had just turned his head away to keep the boy from releasing in his mouth. And was trying to crawl out of the tub but wasn't able to get any further than bent over the edge of it with his butt turned up. Because Ding Ding had slipped on the bar of soap that fell during the scuffle and had come down on the man's back. Somehow, when that happened, the boy's thing, this time, ended up deep inside the man's ass pressing against his prostate gland. Which caused him to yell, "Oh!" When the two women heard that they rushed to where the sound had come from and discovered the situation. As they stood there in shock paralyzed by what they saw they watched the man's yelling change to whimpers. And in a few more strokes, into grunts of pleasure from getting it done to him by the boy. At that point, since it was too late for him to be embarrassed, the man looked up at his wife and told her in gasping breaths of air, "Well, don't just, stand there. Uh, uh. Call my job. Uh, uh. And tell em, I'll be late. Uh, uh..." With his wife seeing that both he and the boy were committed to getting their satisfaction, she closed the bathroom door and went and made the call. After she did, Ken's mother, who was standing beside her, asked, "Well, what are you going to do now?" And the man's wife replied, "What else?, but, wait my turn." "

"Hee, hee, hee... A-h-h-h-h, ha, ha, ha..."

That punch line at the end of the story made Linda roll with unrestrained laughter. Meanwhile the marijuana cigarette that Al was holding between his fingers had gone out he discovered when he went to take another drag on it. He was laughing too as he rolled the flint striker on the   butane lighter with his thumb to get a flame and hit the joint again. Then he poured some more wine into his, almost, empty cup. All the laughter had aroused Butch's curiosity. Causing him to scramble from under the bench and give Al and Linda a couple of friendly barks. And Al said, "You know that shit was funny when it makes somebody's dog laugh." Which only made him and Linda laugh harder. Because it did seem like Butch had a smile on his rough looking dog face. When he saw that nobody was moving to get off the table he went back to his comfortable spot under the bench and continued to watch the basketball game.

The half-court basketball game was on the east side of the gym. And on the north side of it, between it and the swimming pool, were the monkey bars, slide, and merry-go-round a small group of children had occupied. Several women sat on a nearby outside pool bench watching the kids and the game through the lens of their tinted sunglasses. Two men were jogging around the park track. And some people were playing dominos and getting high like Al at another table.

After taking a sip of his wine again, Al leaned back and propped himself using his left arm as a pole. Holding his cup on top of his right leg where it joined with his stomach. In turn, Linda had postured herself in a forward lean with her shoulders arched up and arms straight, gripping the edge of the table on both sides of her. For a moment Al held his lazy sitting position to settle down from the good laugh that he and Linda had just enjoyed together. And while he did that he contemplated on how to follow it up. Then he abandoned his backward sly lean to sit holding his cup with both hands, bent forward, resting his forearms on top of his legs. "Now, what do I get in return for telling you something funny?," he asked her in a pleasant low, but, serious tone.

His question and the way he presented it, quickly drew Linda away from reflecting on the humor in the story she had just been told by Al. But as she turned and glanced at him, she kept smiling. Knowing very well the type of answer he was looking for, he wasn't going to get. It only took a second for her to think of something. Then her smile mischievously broadened as she turned her head again to face him. And looking into his hopeful eyes she answered, "A slice of my homemade apple pie."

"I want some pie alright. But not that kind."

"Yeah, Al. I know that. But this pie tastes a lot better. I g-u-a-r-a-n-t-e-e it! Ha, ha, ha..."

"So, I have to wait until some distant time from now until you decide to bake apple pie, huh."

"No. Because not long before you showed up I baked one. And came over here to sit for a while waiting for it to cool down. Now, wouldn't you really rather have a bit out of it instead of me? Hee, hee, hee..."

"Well now. I see that you've got a few jokes of your own. Not bad in a paradoxical sort of way."

"Because the statement seems to contradict itself, but most likely is true."

"I should have known you'd figure it out with that college edge-joo-moo-cation you got. But yeah. That's right. Just like the story I just told you is. I exaggerated certain parts of it just to make it sound funny. But nonetheless, it's a true story about some murders that happened in the state of Washington back in the nineties."

"Murders? Are you serious?"

"Yeah."

"Then tell me about it Al. Who gets killed?"

"Hold up. Now, you're already in my debt for some apple pie. So. How much deeper in it are you willing to go in order to find out? Say? Some slow dancing and grinding in your daddy's den when nobody's home but you?"

"You don't give up do you?"

"No."

"Well, like they say I guess, 'curiosity killed the cat. But satisfaction brought it back.'"

"Aint that the gospel truth. Aman sister."

"I won't promise you Al. But if the story is good – I might. Now, answer my question. Who gets killed?"

"They all do. The retarded kid, his mother, and the married couple."

Chapter Two
The Real Story

*T*he ceremony at the School For Children With Disabilities was such a big event that many of the parents, friends, and relatives of the young boys and girls who went there were forced to park their vehicles on the residential streets surrounding the school. The closing of car doors, horns honking, and sound of excited voices caused a commotion that stirred up the residents in the normally quiet neighborhood. It just so happened that a married couple who had befriended one of the children at the school were among the people that had come to their livingroom window to see what all the noise and chatter was about. They watched the children stream by dressed in little green caps and gowns, as some of the parents were either telling their child to behave or running to grab a hold of their kid who wanted to play with a friend along the way. Suddenly, the married couple took notice of one of the children who looked familiar. Like the boy they'd given the nickname Ding Ding to. "Honey that looks like Ken," the wife said. "It s-u-r-e does," her husband answered. That made his wife anxious to find out for sure, so she suggested to him that they go out on their front porch before the boy and the woman who was escorting him got past their house. When they opened the front door and walked out on the porch it caught the attention of most of the people passing by including the boy and woman. The married couple gave them a friendly wave, but, looked more directly at the boy than the woman. At first he looked at the man and woman standing on their porch waving at him with a puzzled expression? Then in a few more steps he yanked and excitedly exclaimed, "Them my friends! Stop! Them my friends Momma!" Attempting to get up to where the man and woman were standing. They stood watching helplessly as the boy made a ruckus whining, pulling, and jerking. Until, it occurred to the man to say, "It's true Mam. We're friends of Ken." That gave his mother the idea that it might calm him down if she promised to let him visit his friends coming back from his graduation. And realizing that the man and woman had heard her make that promise, she looked up towards them and pleadingly asked, "Would you mind if we did for a few minutes?" The woman answered, "No, not at all." As her husband gave a reassuring smile and side-to-side head movement that indicated to the boy's mother they were taking full responsibility for the incident.

Around the time that she thought they would be returning from the graduation ceremony, she settled down on her livingroom sofa with a copy of Women's Magazine to preoccupy herself with something while she waited by the window. Not very long after she did small groups of the adults and children began trickling back to where their cars, trucks, and vans were parked. It took awhile, but Ken and his mother were among them. She spotted them coming up the walkway leading to her house. And folded the magazine together and got to the door before there was any chance of a knock. Then opened it with a pleasant smile and said, "Hi."

"Hi. We're back as you can see. I certainly hope it's not a bother."

"Of course not. Please, come in. My husband and I have been looking forward to meeting you."

Just as they stepped into the house and the woman closed the door, her husband walked into the livingroom where they were with a warm smile and said, "Hello." Then his wife, Ding Ding, and his mother seated themselves on the livingroom sofa while he sat down on the adjacent love seat. The boy's mother took the initiative to speak first. "I'm Janis Watson and this is my son Kenny. Apparently, as you already know," she stated.

"And I'm Alice Vargas. And this is my husband Larry. For some time now he and I have been chatting with your son Ken during our exercise walks together whenever we pass by his school and he's at the fence near the sidewalk. We've often wondered who his parents are."

"I'm the only one. I adopted him when he was a baby. I wasn't married. And I'm still not..."

While the two women continued to exchange information and get acquainted Ken sat quietly beside his mother gazing around the livingroom and spotted something, that Larry took notice, Ken seemed to be very interested in. So he politely interrupted Janis, who was explaining some of the details about the graduation ceremony. "Excuse me. I'd like to let Ken take a closer look at whatever it is that he seems to be interested in that's sitting on top of the mantel. That is, if you don't mind letting him come over with me?" Immediately Janis' attention was drawn to her son and she saw that he was scooting up to the edge of the sofa, indicating to her that indeed he wanted to get off of it and do what Larry had told her. Janis hesitated for a second then she said, "Alright," as she swiveled her legs to let Ken get past her in between the sofa and coffee table. "Behave yourself," she added, as her son hurried to get along side of Larry to walk with him over to the fireplace. Once there, Larry found out that it was the picture of a young boy sitting on top of a large rock that Ken was interested in. He wanted to know where the boy was? And could he go play with him? "Well, maybe?," Larry said pulling a gag on Ken. He got a personal laugh out it for a second, until it became obvious that he had to tell the retarded kid the truth. "You see, that's me when I was about your age," Larry told him as they sat on the carpet musing at the photograph. "That big rock I'm sitting on is called a boulder." He went on to tell young Ken that he was at summer camp then. And explained to him a little bit about camping. That you explore the woods, fish, make campfires, sleep in tents and sleeping bags...

The pow-wow that the man and boy were having ended when Ken overheard his mother telling Alice about his aunt Kathy and uncle David. That she has a married sister with three children that also live in the area. When he heard that and saw his mother pulling out the pictures of them that she carried in her wallet, Ken quickly lost interest in what Larry was telling him and scrambled back to her side. As soon as that happened Larry stood up and put the picture of himself back on the mantel and went over to join in with everyone. It was quite a surprise to he and his wife to see Ken take center stage naming everyone that his mother showed a picture of and explain what was going on at that particular time. They had no idea that a retarded person, a kid especially, could have that kind of memory and wit. In response to the exasperated expression on their faces, Janis said, "As you can see the only real problem that my son has is being stuck with the mind of a six year old." And under her breath added, "And unable to eat certain things." The married couple took that as a sign it was worth her to mention it but nothing that she cared to go into any details about. Silence followed. Then Janis took advantage of it by saying, "Well, we've got to be getting on our way now." In return, Alice knew as a good hostess it was her duty to politely agree. And said, "OK then. My husband and I really enjoyed your visit." And Larry gave a supportive nod of his head. "I hope it won't be the last one. After all, we practically live around the corner from each other," Alice said to convince Janis that she was sincere.

"Yes, that is true. But of course, I wouldn't want to drop by unexpectedly. Why don't we exchange numbers?"

"Yeah. Why don't we? I'd love for us to stay in touch."

After they did everyone stood, headed to the front door, then bid each other goodbye.

Chapter Three
The Nevada Days

*G*rowing up, Janis and her younger sister Kathy were always close. They often were mistaken for twins, but weren't. Because, they were born one year apart. Their father, Harold Watson, was a hotel casino manager in Reno, Nevada. And was a very smart man. But his wife Ginger was the one between him and her who had the better set of brains. She'd grown up in New York and majored in business in college. She met Harry while vacationing and visiting some relatives of hers that lived in Reno, because, she didn't want to leave there without having some fun on her last night in one of the casinos. And ended up at Club Paradise. There were a lot of exciting gambling choices inside but what she decided on was blackjack because she and her best friend Margie played that a lot with each other. As it just so happened to turn out that night Harry was working the table she sat down at. And he milked her wallet nearly bone dry of every bit of cash she had in it, plus, what she borrowed. But it was fortunate for her he'd fallen in love with her in the process of that. And that, the casino had a policy that gave dealers the discretion to let some customers win back a portion of their losses. It was that and his smooth conversation that got him in bed with Ginger later that night. That's when she got pregnant. And of course, didn't find that out until she got back to New York. And just lucky for Janis, after Ginger told Marg about it, she convinced Ginger to at least try to get in touch with Harry to discuss it with him before she went through with her plans to have an abortion.

When he got the news, Harry was ecstatic. And made arrangements to fly to New York immediately. He got there and wined and dined Ginger for three wonderful days at the Ritz Hotel. Then he got down on his knees and opened a little red box. And she didn't need any more convincing than that. The next morning they were on their way back to Reno to get married. It paid off for Harry because Ginger coached him on ways to get promoted and invest his earnings in stock shares of the Paradise. By the time that Kathy graduated from high school he co-owned enough shares of the hotel chain to cash in and go into business for himself. And he opened the Duce's Wild Night Club and Casino. And that's when the money really started to roll in for him and Ginger. After Harry opened the club Janis and Kathy started college. But dropped out after they auditioned and got a job working for their parents. They managed to pull it off because they had a lot of showgirl friends. And used the knowledge they gained from them to secretly develop their own act. "Twist" and "Shout." The crowd always loved it. They were hot.

What spoiled it for all of them was the fact that the wrong people began to notice, just how much money Harry's business operation was actually making. And the fact that he was an independent entrepreneur. A loner. Merely a small piranha swimming in an ocean of great white sharks. In other words, he was vulnerable for a corporate take over. From his experience, he knew what that meant. How nasty things could get if he didn't cooperate. At any time he might be struck by lightening, a satellite from outer-space, or fall into the bottomless pit of a deserted mine shaft somewhere in the Nevada hills or desert. Or even worse, his dentist might run out of aesthetic while pulling his teeth. He had no doubt that things could happen to him that no insurance policy would cover. But like they say, 'behind every cloud lies a silver lining.' And Harry's was in the fact that he was respected and liked by the old schools who remembered how he'd played along with them by acting like he didn't know about things that mattered when the heat was on. But still, he understood that there were limits. Ginger's advice was for him to keep negotiating and renegotiating while his profits continued to pump up the price of shares. Then sell at their peak to the highest bidder. And he followed that advice and walked away a very rich man. And Ginger, a very wealthy woman.

If they had wanted to, Janis and Kathy could have lived comfortably off of what their parents had offered to give them. But they chose not to because they felt like they'd been paid enough in salary. And by, Harry and Ginger raising them. They both had lived rent free and had saved the majority of the money they had earned. So instead of traveling around the country with their parents, made the decision to stay in Reno and start over from scratch. Which didn't seem hard to do to either one of them. Because they had grown up there, had a lot of contacts, and most importantly, knew their way around.

The Separation

Like the old adage goes, "boys will be boys," and "girls will be girls." And Janis and Kathy weren't even close to being an exception. They partied their ass's off. Not in the ordinary sense. But extraordinary one. Jet-setting to private parties given by people like Player Boy, Big Comedy and those Arab Sheiks who'll invest as much as 20 million dollars on a horse just for the thrill of having the opportunity to race it in the Kentucky Derby. For almost a year after Harry and Ginger signed over the deed of their home to them, that's all Janis and Kathy did. But it wasn't just fun and games. It was work too. Because on nearly all of those occasions the reason for them being wherever they were was to help entertain the guests of whoever was throwing the party. That's how they made their living. But at the same time it's why they ended up going their separate ways.

It all got started with Cynthia Wells. A showgirl from out of town who met Janis and Kathy at a party they were giving themselves. Emma Russell, who had worked for their parents and had become a good friend of Janis and Kathy, had been invited to their party and brought Cynthia with her. She had been doing shows at the Century in Las Vegas up until she got spotted by a high roller named Jake Malloy. Jake made arrangements to be introduced to Cynthia backstage after one of the shows. Then after they met and everything went smooth he invited her to join him on his yacht, and that led to her eventually jet-setting with him to a lot of places. Including Reno, Nevada where Emma had just started working at the Gold Mine. Cynthia ended up there with Jake for a one and a-half million dollar poker tournament. But she got bored on the first day and decided while Jake was busy trying to stack his chips that she would ask around and find out whether the place needed another showgirl. And by coincidence, they did need another extra and hired her on the spot. The job was only temporary of course, until Jake cashed in his chips. But that took two or three more days. During that time is when Emma and Cynthia met and became friends. And they went to the house party that Janis and Kathy had thrown. As the party wore on all four of the girls had a chance to sit down and hold a conversation outside on the patio in front of the swimming pool. Naturally Cynthia had to tell something about herself. And she did. Plus, a lot more. Emma was impressed but Janis and Kathy were fascinated. Convinced by Cynthia that they could make a lot of money doing their 'twist and shout' thing at private jet-set parties. Hanging out with movie stars, sports celebrities, and recording artist. She told them, "That video you showed of your act would probably make you a lot of money in the right hands. But I'm positive you could do it performing live on the jet-set. Because it's a hot act and both of you are sexy as hell. And look good. That's in demand all over the world. Even in China." And true to her word, Cynthia introduced them to Jake before they jetted out of town together.

Eventually, the inevitable happened. Janis and Kathy were made offers that they couldn't refuse. Janis's was making movies in Europe. And Kathy's was getting married to a high roller.

Chapter Four
Making Strange Bedfellows

*I*t was a cold early Saturday morning in the winter of 1996 when Alice arrived at Janis's house in Seattle's capital hill district to have breakfast. She thought that it would be a good idea to do it at iHOP since Ken was coming along. But Janis wanted to eat somewhere a little more upscale than that. "I like the International House of Pancakes, but know of a better place, she told Alice. "OK. Where?," she asked.

"Eggs Et Cetra."

"I've never heard of them."

"Well, maybe that's because nobody's ever mentioned it to you before. But you've passed by it at least a thousand times I'm sure. Just without noticing."

"Where is it?"

"On Broadway."

"On Broadway?"

"Yeah. Just off of Olive. Come on. I'll show you. Ken, are you ready?"

"Yes. I'm ready momma."

After breakfast the three of them returned and while Janis and Alice sat together in the kitchen chit-chatting, Ken settled down in his room to watch cartoons. It was a little more than two years into their friendship and both women had gotten very comfortable exchanging personal information with each other. But something had been avoided. At least, up to that point it had. "Hey, how 'bout some chilled wine to go with this good conversation we're having?," asked Janis. "Sounds like a winner to me. What-cha got?," replied Alice.

"A bottle of Chaplin Brother's vintage white 1990. You'll like it just as much as you did eating breakfast at Eggs Et Cetra this morning."

"We have a lot of 'first things' going on today. I'm wondering is there something else that we can add to it?"

As Janis put the bottle of wine and glasses on the table and sat down she answered, "Well now that I think about it, maybe there is?"

"What?"

"You telling me why you didn't finish college. I've always been curious about what made you quit? Is it too personal for you to tell me?"

"No. Not anymore, I guess..."

****

It was during spring break. And Alice was riding in Karen's car with Ashley and Bridget parading down Ocean Front Boulevard with other carloads of college students who were out late that night to have a good time partying. The skimpy clothing the girls wore in the warm Florida weather revealed all of their secret assets. And Alice, in particular, had some pretty nice ones to look at. "Hey! You ought to be a stripper!," someone in the crowd of bystanders yelled at her. "Me? Become a floor wax remover? Nothing doing baby!," she yelled back with a haughty smile on her face. Everyone in the crowd who overheard the exchange burst into cheerful laughter. Including the man who had come on to her. His name was Blake Pantera. He was the owner of a popular strip club in the Miami Beach area that he'd named the Black Panther after himself. And considered Alice's remark to be a challenge. So he maneuvered his way through the crowd following the slow moving convertible until he was slightly ahead of it, then he stepped out from among the people standing at the edge of the curb and flagged the car down. What made Karen want to stop more than anything else was the Steven Segal look he had, that, except of his shorter height, made him easily mistaken for the actor. She, as well as Ashley, Bridget and Alice, were mesmerized by the resemblance. "Hey, I want to apologize," he said stepping up to the passenger's side of the BMW making eye contact with Karen. "I'm the guy who made that remark back there to your friend here," said as he smoothly switched his attention from Karen to Alice. And before either one of them could respond he continued, by saying, "Please allow me to introduce myself. My name is Blake Pantera. Welcome to Miami Beach. I noticed the out-of-state license plate," he quickly added. "I own a club here in town named the Black Panther and would like for all of you to come there tonight after this street party is over and be my special guests. Just follow the crowd and you won't have any problem finding it. Tell the doorman that I personally invited you to come. And when he asks you for the password say BMW." Then he pushed off from the car and stepped back into the crowd, confident that they would locate someone to follow and show up at his place.

Rather than wait in the long line that was outside of the club the girls were smart enough to cut to the chase by giving the bouncer who was stationed in front of the club the information they had. When it cleared over his headset he held up his arm and signaled to the doorman to let them through ahead of everyone else.

Outside the club there was every kind of foreign sports car you could name. And the most expensive American made ones too. People were bumping their sound systems, cruising around slowly trying to find a spot to pull into to park. While others were just leaning against the side of their ride or the grill of it high signing their wheels and paint job and the way that they were dressed. It was another kind of party all within itself. But inside the club was where the real action was at.

As soon as they got inside, all four of the girls felt the seductive effects of the jungle-like atmosphere and enormity of the place. The vibration of the comfortably loud music and mixture of perfume and alcohol smells were intoxicating. They saw an ocean of bodies dancing and mingling together in sync. And the sight of it turned on their own individual freaky urge to make physical contact with the opposite sex. They got wet. As the animal instincts inside of them surged between their legs silently turning them into wildcats that wanted to be tamed.

It was only a short wait in the lobby for them before being escorted to a reserved table. Not on the ground floor, but upstairs where each one was separated by a partition overlooking everything below. They were told by the waiter that their drinks were on the house and anything to eat if they wanted something. And asked what would they like to order. After placing them they were advised that the owner would be coming soon. Then the waiter said, "I'll have your drinks brought up very shortly." They were all smiles. And very talkative when the waiter left.

None of them had any idea that Blake hadn't showed up at their table yet because he was busy calculating a diplomatic approach to getting Alice off by herself. Time was of the essence and he couldn't keep the girls waiting on him much longer. Finally, he decided that he didn't have any other choice but to call Kelly. Kelly Nash was one of Blake's managers. Or, one of his right-hand men, is a better way of putting it. He relied on her to handle delicate situations—like the one he was in. Because she was the kind of woman who could step down into a pit of rattlesnakes, charm every last one of them out of their skin, and never get bit even after they woke up to the fact that she'd done that. "Well Blake. Since you don't know them the first thing is to sit down with them and get familiar enough to call each one by their first name. Which shouldn't take but a few minutes since there's only four of them. Actually, three, considering that remembering the girl's name that you're interested in will automatically stick in your mind. While you're doing that I'll have a table cleared on the floor so the other three are accessible. Then you escort them to it, excuse yourself for a brief moment, and return and whisper in that girl's ear you want to introduce her to someone. Then bring her to me. And I'll handle it for you from there." And just like Kelly anticipated, as soon as the girls were seated on the ground floor they started getting those 'hey, let's-get-acquainted looks' by a lot of handsome well dressed guys that were on the prowl. Making it easy for Blake to sweep Alice away alone with him.

Just seconds after that, Karen, Ashley, and Bridget one-by-one themselves disappeared into the quicksand of swaying, dipping, and jerking bodies that were moving to the dance music.

While Kelly sat in her office waiting she knew that getting Alice there was the easy part. But convincing her to work for Blake as a stripper would be more difficult. Especially in one encounter. What made it even more of a challenge was the fact that Alice was a college student. "OK," she thought to herself. "Changing the girl's opinion, her concept of strippers, is one half. Motivating her to get involved is the other half.

And finding the right tools to make them fit together smoothly is what I'm trying to do here. Alright. I'm the right tool for the first thing. But who is for the second?," she wondered for a moment. Then blurted, "Cee Cee." And pressed the speed-dial on her phone to get in touch with her downstairs in her dressing room before she went on stage. Kelly ordered her to cancel her act. And explained why...

After Blake introduced them to each other he left Alice alone with Kelly in her office. "Well Alice, I wanted to meet you personally because Blake explained what happened at the block-party earlier tonight. And he didn't feel like his mere apology and invitation for you and your friends to enjoy yourselves at his club, free-of-charge, was adequate. So, I offered to help him with his problem. And that is, to eliminate any misconception you may have gotten, not only about his comment, but also, about any you may have formulated prior to that about the stripping profession itself." Alice sat there spellbound by every word that came out of Kelly's viperous mouth. "First, Blake's true and only intention was to compliment your extraordinary beauty. And second, he wanted to offer you an employment opportunity in a profession that pays women a higher salary than the vast majority of people with college degrees make after they graduate. Doing a lot less work. And having a lot more fun. I mean, just think about how much fun you were having when Blake yelled at you. His point was, why show off what you have for nothing? Why not reward yourself with a lot more than just guys whistling and yelling at you? Doesn't it make good sense to do that? Get paid thousands of dollars for it, on top of having that kind of fun?" Alice knew that she had a dilemma. Because to answer no, would be utterly ridiculous. And to answer yes, would be putting herself in a position, that, would no doubt be an embarrassment and great disappointment to her parents. Who had worked hard for the money they saved to put her through college. Kelly saw Alice mentally struggling to find the right answer and knew it was time to put part two of her scheme in action. Immediately. "Look Alice. I'm not trying to get you to fill out an application. All I'm trying to do is open your eyes to certain realities. That's all."

"I understand."

"Good. I'm glad to hear that. Tell you what. How 'bout a tour backstage to meet one of the girls? Would you be OK with that?"

"Sure."

"Alright then. Follow me."

Kelly led Alice to Cee-Cee's dressing room. Introduced them. And left for over an hour.

****

Alice's story was interrupted for a brief moment when Ken walked in the kitchen and asked Janis could he go over to his aunt Kathy and uncle David's house to visit his cousins. She told him yes. But that it would be later on after she and Alice were through talking. He said, "Alright," with a disappointing frown on his face. And walked away. As he went, Janis suggested, "Why don't you take a nap honey? And we'll go when you wake up. OK?" She got no response as he made his way out of sight. Then she casually turned back towards Alice and asked her, "So, what did you and Cee Cee talk about for that hour you were left in her dressing room until Kelly returned and took you back to where your friends were?"

"About the business. How much money she makes and how much I could. She encouraged me to try on a couple of her outfits. And I did. We had fun. I guess what really made me decide to work there and quit college was her convincing me that I could pay my parents everything back in one or two months. And that, even her parents were disappointed. But chilled out when they saw how well she was doing financially. After that, they let her live her own life. And she said that mine would eventually do the same thing."

"Did it work out that way?"

"Well, to a certain extent it did. I was able to pay my parents their money back alright. But right after that I ended up getting into some serious trouble."

"What? For drugs or something?"

"No. Something much more serious than that. A murder charge."

"You're kidding right?"

"No. I'm serious. What happened was, I shot Cee Cee's ex-boyfriend and killed him. But in self defense. You see, Cee Cee and I got real close. And decided to share an apartment together. A penthouse. Greg, didn't like that. Because he wasn't in the picture anymore. And he wasn't because Cee Cee was tired of him spending all of her money on coke and throwing wild parties for his beer-belly friends. He accused me of being, quote, "A man-stealing lesbian bitch." And late one night in the club's employee parking lot, he came out of nowhere and attacked me while Cee Cee and I were sitting in her Corvette deciding whether to go straight home or hang out somewhere. He busted out the window on my side of the car with a little league baseball bat and tried to drag me out and beat me with it. The only thing that saved me was grabbing the gun we kept in the glove compartment for protection and blasting Greg with it before he got to me."

"Did they let you go since you killed the guy in self defense?"

"No. I had to go to prison."

"Why? That doesn't make any sense."

"I went because, the prosecuting attorney introduced the theory to the jury that I shot Greg in the parking lot once in the chest, which brought him down and disabled him. But she claimed that I stood over him after that and shot him again in the head to make sure he was dead. My attorney argued that even if that were true, I acted out of fear and the instinct to protect myself from being attacked again. And in the heat of the moment, wasn't particular about where the gun was pointing. So, based on that the jury had two choices. Second degree murder or manslaughter. And lucky for me they chose the lesser charge of manslaughter. Instead of murder. Otherwise, I would still be in prison."

"How long were you in there?"

"Five years."

"That's a long time. How did you manage to survive?"

"By doing what I had to do. Playing the same game that everyone else was. Keeping quiet."

"Does that mean that you had to, well, you know?"

"What? Have sex with other women?"

"Well, yeah. Did you?"

"I guess the best way to answer that question is to ask, what would you have done in that exact same situation?"

It was pretty clear to Janis that, indirectly, Alice was admitting to her of having a lesbian relationship while she was in prison. And it was also obvious to her that the answer she gave to Alice's question was going to define the relationship they were going to have with each other from that point forward. So with hardly any hesitation she responded, "Probably the same thing that you did." They both smiled and giggled a little bit. Then Janis added, "Well, it's nothing to be ashamed of. Women do it all the time. Look at Elaine and Rose Mary. And all of the others photographed kissing each other at night clubs. You know they do it to let everybody know they've done more than that and enjoyed it." Alice was in full agreement with Janis about that, but, she was dissatisfied. Because Janis hadn't confessed her sins. And before she realized it, had bluntly asked her, "So, when was your first time?" Janis was caught off guard by that and stumbled. "Uh, mine?"

"Yeah. We're not playing head games are we?"

"No. It's just, you surprised me. I wasn't expecting you to be so direct, since, I hadn't been with you. That's all."

"Ooops. My bag. Sorry about that. But I figured, why continue to be evasive with each other now that everything is out in the open?"

"You're right. Well, like you, I went to college for awhile. But wanted to get into the sorority there. Without knowing what I'd be put through. Anyway. Poor little ole me was still a virgin. And it got around."

"Wait a minute. You were still a virgin when you started going to college?"

"Yeah."

"OK. Now let me ask you the same question that you asked me? And that is, 'How did you manage that?' "

"Very carefully. Ha, ha, ha..."

"With toys huh."

"No. Just my middle finger and a good imagination. That's all. But to make a long story short, I was raped by three senior girls with the help of two senior guys. They set up this bogus call to my dorm that summoned me to the school library late one night. When I got there and spoke with the clerk about it that's when I found out the call was a prank. I left the library thinking nothing else about it when suddenly I was grabbed from behind and dragged into the bushes in the rear of the building. One of the guys had his hand over my mouth so I couldn't scream and his other arm around my upper body, while his accomplice had me by my legs. I said they dragged me but I was carried. To a clearing between the building and bushes where the three girls were waiting with a blanket spread on the ground. The guy that had his hand over my mouth grabbed me around my throat with it and choked me to force my mouth open so the girls could gag me. You know, like those guys were done in that movie

Real Fiction. Then they laid me on the blanket and pulled off my clothes from the waist down. They were smart and waited until I was so tired I couldn't struggle anymore if I wanted to. Then the girls took turns eating me out. Playing a sort of musical chair game with my pussy to see which one would get caught licking it when I came."

"W-o-o-w. Did you like it?"

"Not at first. But the more they did it, I just got to the point where all I could do was moan."

"So, it wasn't until later that you found out that, that was your initiation."

"Yeah."

"Well, what about the other way around? Have you ever tried that? Doing what they did to you to someone in return?"

"Are you asking me that for the reason I think you are?"

"Maybe."

"Uh– let me check on Ken."

"OK."

Chapter Five
The Freak Accident

It was Saturday afternoon, and as usual, Larry got out of bed and found his wife gone. After tossing back the covers and slipping on his house coat and shoes he moseyed down the hall to the bathroom, splashed water on his face, then rinsed his mouth and looked into the mirror at himself. "OK. Some coffee and a look at the newspaper first. Then work. Get ready for work," he uttered. When he got to the kitchen he saw the note laying on the table but didn't read it until after his coffee was on. "Gone to Jan's. Be back in time for you to go to work." He left the note in its place, got up and walked out to grab the newspaper off the porch or somewhere nearby it.

Subconsciously Larry had noticed something else besides his newspaper that didn't register until after he picked it up complaining to himself, "On the grass again." Then he took a deliberate stare watching in amazement. "No. It can't be," he told himself. But it was. Ding Ding walking across the playing field of Yesler Park pulling a toy wagon.

The backside of the park could be entered and exited on Nye Street. The street that Larry and Alice lived on. Even though it dead ended. Because the sidewalk was paved leading down into the park. Catacorner to it was where the school was located that Ken had attended and graduated from. Yesler ran east and west in the central district of Seattle. And around that time there was a Silvester Stallone movie being shot in the area. So many of the streets had been temporarily blocked off. Including Yesler. But other streets were on that day. Dam near all of downtown.

Once Larry had gotten Ken inside he was able to find out that the boy wanted to be taken by him to his cousin's house. Saying, his mother wouldn't do it after he asked her about it again. Because she said that she was busy. That's all Larry was able to make out. Except that, his wife had been at the house with his mother talking when he went to sleep, but she wasn't there when he woke up. Then his telephone ranged. "Hello."

"Larry. I'm with Janis. We're downtown at the police station filling out a missing person's report because we can't find Ken."

"He's here with me. I don't know how he managed to do it, but he walked here. Pulling his little red toy wagon behind him. Where did you go when you left Janis' house?"

"Left her house?"

"Yeah. He said he took a nap and when he woke up you were gone."

"No. I've been with her at the house all the time. He probably thought that because I used her bathroom. And was in there quite a while. Because we drank some wine and it gave me diarrhea. But, now that I think about it, you're right. I did go somewhere."

"Where?"

"I drove to the drugstore to get something to take for it."

"Are you alright now?"

"Yeah."

"Good. How soon can you get here? I have to start getting ready for work. And can't do it with Ken on my hands."

"I know. Wait. Hold on honey. There's a police officer trying to get everyone's attention. It sounds important... Larry he just told everybody that we're stuck here for maybe an hour because they're about to shoot another movie scene. So all the streets that the movie people need to use have been closed down. We can't leave the building he said because it might interfere with them making the shot."

"Aint that a bitch."

"Maybe you should go ahead and do as much as you can with Ken there just in case it takes a little longer than that for us to get out of here? And call your job to let 'em know that you might be late because of all this."

"Dam! OK. I will."

Larry decided that since he had plenty of time at the moment he would go ahead with his normal routine and have a few cups of coffee while he mulled over the Seattle Times. He gave the cartoon section to Ken and let him entertain himself with it while he did that. In the meantime. As soon as Alice got off the phone she told Janis, Ken was at her house with Larry and everything was alright. Janis wanted to be angry at her son for running off like that but she couldn't bring herself to do it because she knew that it had been her fault that he had. And Alice felt that same way. That she was the blame. But they kept those thoughts to themselves as they walked together back to the complaint department of the police station to cancel the missing persons report they filed. Finally, everyone was given permission to leave and were told that traffic was jammed. But not that it was due to a detour sign problem. People couldn't figure out which were the right signs for them to follow in order to get where they wanted to go. So Alice got confused because she couldn't drive out of downtown the same way that she'd driven in. And ended up north of Seattle in Ballard. After finding that out Larry knew that he didn't have any choice but to start making his own lunch rather than wait on his wife to do it for him like she normally does.

It had been a long time since Ken had eaten something and when he saw Larry making his lunch sandwiches and packing cookies for desert Ken told him that he was hungry and asked him could he have some. Since the boy wanted to eat something, Larry got the bright idea that, that was a good way for him to keep Ken occupied while he took his shower. So he dug out a t.v. dinner tray and sat it in the bathroom. Then he closed the lid on the toilet seat, had Ken sit on it, and gave him a can of soda pop to go with his cookies because he was out of milk. Then he stepped into the shower, pulled the curtain, disrobed, and began to bathe.

At first, Larry peeped out on Ken every few seconds. But stopped it altogether once he was satisfied that the boy would behave while he finished taking his shower. And he did, until the sugar in the Sweet Treat cookies and can of Zing took their effects on him. Then, suddenly, he began to take on the characteristics of a zombie. Quietly creeping out of all his clothes. His skin darkened and began to drip with perspiration with each mummy-like step he took towards the bathtub. Then he stood in silence at the curtain attempting to call Larry's name but nothing came out of his mouth. Because his brain was overloaded with chaos.

Inside the shower Larry was completely oblivious to what was happening outside of it. The water felt so relaxing rushing out of the spout massaging the top of his head and face with his eyes closed. Then without warning his contentment was abruptly disturbed when he heard the shower curtain snap back, making a zip and crack sound. That both startled and frightened him. His head turned quickly and simultaneously his eyes popped open. Then a bizarre flash of panic rushed into him that accelerated his heart so sudden and rapidly he was subdued by sharp clinching chest pains. The sight of Ken had completely immobilized him in shock. Looking like Mic Jason in "The Dead Walks." His eyes were watery, red, and hypnotic. He was naked and had an exceptionally large penis for his age that was erect. And he was forcing his way into the tub appearing to Larry to be reaching for him with a demonic frown on his face. All Larry could do was let out a squeal and draw back against the shower wall.

Meanwhile. Alice took an alternate route by hitting I- 99 instead if Interstate-5. It was the scenic route that took her and Janis down the coastline. There was far less traffic for her to deal with on it than there would have been had she taken I-5. And in no time she cruised past the Farmer's Market that sat above the pier-front restaurants, shops, and ferry dock. She took the Jackson Street exit and hit 20ᵗʰ, made a left to Nye, and was home a lot sooner than expected. And no sooner than she and Janis walked through the front door they heard, "Oh!" And a thud noise come from the bathroom. They both rushed there. And could not believe what they saw. Larry laying naked on his back with legs bent at the knees, arms stretched out, and his head turned and eyes squinched closed. With Ken laying face down on top of him, just beginning to roll off on his side. They watched as the boy's penis slowly softened and shrunk to its normal size. Then Alice burst into tears. Crying shamefully. And was so embarrassed that she ran into her bedroom, slammed the door, and hid in the closet. While Janis reacted by gathering up Ken's clothes and taking him into the living room to get dressed. Then she called Kathy to pick her up.

Larry himself got dressed. And while he did, had no luck with getting Alice to come out of the bedroom closet. Even though Janis was gone. But before she had, he'd spoken with her about the peculiar situation that he was caught in by she and his wife with her retarded son. "I tried to get him out of the shower but he was determined not to let me do it Janis. While I struggled with him the bar of soap I was using fell in the tub and I stepped on it, twisted, and fell backwards. Instinctively I grabbed a hold of Ken trying to regain my balance and we both ended up outside of the tub with the wind knocked out of us. That's why, for a minute or two, I couldn't move."

"I understand. And I'm sure Alice will too once she calms down. But, you know she's gonna wonder, just like I am right now, why you gave Ken all of that sweet stuff to eat after I had made it clear that under no circumstances was he to be fed anything with large amounts of sugar in it?"

"But you never explained why Janis. And that was so long ago that I just forgot about it."

Since there was nothing that could be done medically, when Kathy arrived in her mini-van to pick up her sister and nephew she drove them straight home. But left there with Ken in the car. She took him home with her.

Chapter Six

*L*arry worked in West Seattle at SeaLand as a security guard. He had the six-to-two night shift and drove up to the security gate to relieve Russ, right on schedule. "Hey Russ," Larry said, as he slowly came to a stop in front of the open door of the guardhouse. His voice was weak as he stretched out his left arm to grab the time card that Russ was handing to him. "I thought you'd be about an hour late coming in from the way it sounded when word got to me that your wife had the car and was being held as a hostage by the people making that Stallone movie," Russ jokingly told Larry. Ker plunk!, went the time clock as he pushed his time card in. "Yeah, I probably would have if she had taken I-5 instead of 99," Larry responded as he handed his time card back to Russ to put back in its place. "You don't sound to good Larry. Is something wrong?," Russ inquired.

"Yeah. My back is killing me. I slipped taking my shower in a hurry to make it here on time. And now I'm really starting to feel it."

"Well, I can stand in for you tonight. I need some extra hours. You want me to get a hold of Vick?"

"Yeah. Because I won't be worth a dime around here if I stay."

"OK. Go ahead and pull through."

Victor Gibbson was the man in charge of the guards working at SeaLand for Diamond. The security company that had been contracted to protect the property, trucks, and merchandise that was delivered and shipped. He was standing on the loading dock when Russ beeped him. He checked the number and saw that the call had come from Guard

House1, then stepped inside of the warehouse and called back from the office. "Tell Larry I said it's OK. He can take a couple of sick-leave days off if he needs to."

As soon as Russ cleared several vehicles to pass through the check point he signaled for Larry to drive his car back through. "The boss told me to tell you that its OK to take a couple of sick-leave days off if you need to."

"Thanks Russ."

"Hey. No problem. See you when you get better."

Larry punched out on sick-leave then drove across the West Seattle bridge and hit Swift, taking it to the top of Beacon Hill, and drove north on Beacon heading for Harbor View Medical Center's emergency clinic. He registered in, got checked, and left.

While he waited for the stoplight on 12th and Borden to change he decided that there were just too many complications waiting for him at home to go back there. So when the light changed he veered left at the next intersection and hit Rainier. At first he was just driving with no particular place in mind to go, but as he approached McClullen the name La Villa on the motel sign caught his attention, and he decided to pull in and rent a room there. As soon as he got inside of it he plopped down on the queen-size bed and stared into the ceiling ... Finally, he picked up the phone and called home. The line was busy. So he went outside to his car and brought in his sack lunch and put it in the refrigerator. He waited a few more minutes then dialed again. This time the phone rang but there was no answer. He left a message.

While he laid on top of the bed letting his mind wonder he remembered seeing a bar that was just up the street from the motel. And thought to himself, "That's exactly what I need right now. A drink." So he took a walk to the place. And ironically, when he stepped into the dim-lit bar the jukebox was playing, "Aint That A Bitch," by Johnny Guitar Watson. He noticed there were only a few people inside and saw the stools were all empty at the far end of the bar counter. And made a decision to sit there in one of them. As soon as he sat down the bartender, eager to please his new patron, quickly moved over to Larry and said, "Hello friend. What's your pleasure?"

"Well for starters, I'll have a Jack Daniels and pitcher of Budweiser."

"Coming right up!"

After paying for his drinks he sat for a long moment with his head down. Then he raised it in an 'oh what-the-hell' fashion and emptied the glass of whisky in one gulp and began chasing it down with a glass of Bud. Without paying any attention to who was watching him.

While Alice waited at her livingroom window for her cab to arrive she and Janis were on the phone talking to each other. Then she hung up and left when it came. "Where to Miss?," the cab driver asked her once she adjusted herself in the backseat. "Eleven-seventeen Pine."

Alice walked up the steps and rang the doorbell. Then waited in the porch light on the step for the door to open. A few seconds later she was inside. Janis greeted her with a warm smile and loose embrace that was accompanied by a tender kiss on the lips. They separated, Alice hung her coat on the rack in the foyer, then followed Janis into the den. They sat close together facing each other on the leather sofa, as the burning wood crackled in the fireplace. "On my way over I got a voice message from Larry. He went to work but didn't stay. Instead he rented a motel room at the Villa down on Rainier," Alice mentioned right off. "Well, I'm glad you decided to spend the night here with me instead of at home alone, at a time like this. I feel so much of the blame for what happened today. Alice I'm really sorry," Janis said, sympathetically.

"Really, you don't have to be. Because Larry lied to you about what happened. At least, I believe he did, anyway. Based on what I know about his past."

****

In school Larry excelled and was always at the top of his class. Which, during his senior year in high school helped him to earn money as a teacher's aid. Tutoring other students. One of them was Juan Rodriguez. Juan was street-smart. And didn't like wasting his time sitting in a classroom just to get an A or B put on a piece of paper. He'd rather pay someone to have that done for him. And Larry turned out to be that someone. It so happened that Juan, in the meantime, was connected with some big time drug traffickers of marijuana and cocaine. And not long after he persuaded Larry to do his class work for money he saw Larry's potential to do it for free, plus, help him sell drugs. So, his next move on his chessboard was to introduce Larry to marijuana. He got Larry high on it. Then he set up a small clientele for him to sell the stuff to, showing him that he could make three or four times the money that he was getting paid in cash. And when he saw that Larry could handle his business Juan began selling coke and grass to him direct. When Juan graduated from high school business for Larry on college campus was good. But in 'that' business, all it takes is one mistake. And unfortunately, Larry made several. The first, was trying to cut Juan out of the picture and buy more product at a cheaper price from someone else. The second, was not knowing it was a corrupt drug enforcement agent that was offering him the better deal. And the third and final mistake, was Larry attempting to rat on Juan to get out of the mess. Because Juan's connections were as big as Pablo Escobar and it was them who had set everything up with the agent to test him. To find out if he was truly solid or not before they let him handle their merchandise in bulk quantities. When Larry failed the test the agent flipped the script by turning the fake arrest into a real bust. And made Larry believe that he was getting a deal by pleading guilty to state charges rather than federal ones because he'd do less time. It definitely was a good deal in that sense. But it cost Larry his manhood. Because he went to prison with a snitch jacket on him. So his ass was property of the Mexican mafia as soon as he stepped off the chain bus. Eventually, Larry got wise and checked into protective custody. But he was a bag of damaged goods by then. A 'recovering homosexual' is the way he phrased it in the first letter he wrote to Alice. They met while she was in prison for the manslaughter conviction through the Jim Bakker pen pal ministry. It was just a coincidence that during that time Larry and Alice were drawn to Jim's message and wrote letters to him for prayers to find a companion to help change their lifestyles. And miraculously the ministry paired them together. Little by little they shared more about themselves to each other and over a period of time discovered the friendship they began had transcended into love. When Alice got out she found work in San Francisco and waited on Larry. And when he got out they moved to Seattle and married.

****

While Alice sat in Janis' den giving her the low-down on Larry's past, he sat inside the shady bar meditating over his half-full glass of beer wondering how could Ken have been left unattended so long before Janis and his wife discovered that he was gone? Meanwhile the alcohol had began taking its affect and forced him to desire a more comfortable position than he was in on the stool he was sitting. So he collected his drink and moved from the bar counter to a table, sat down, and slumped to one side in his chair. Then, before he knew it, someone was standing at his table politely saying, "Excuse me. If you don't mind I'd like to ask you a question."

In the meantime, Alice concluded her story by telling Janis, "So, I think that Larry deliberately gave Ken all that sweet stuff to eat knowing very well what would happen, because he'd done it before somewhere along the line and found out. Maybe during those camp outings he's taken Ken on with him a few times? And if what you say is true about Ken's mind blanking out whenever that happens, that explains why we've never known about it until today."

"That dirty bastard! I could kill him for taking advantage of my son like that!," Janis said angrily before she knew it. "And I could too. The sight of him getting it done to him by a thirteen year old retarded boy was so disgusting," Alice replied broken heartedly.

Chapter Seven
Four Dead Bodies

There were four stiff bodies laying in the morgue. Detective Bryant Ferguson was co-assigned to investigate the death of the adolescent boy. "Chief, what I've been able to gather from the police report, is that, the kid, Kenneth Watson, spent the night with his cousins. And apparently he got up in the middle of the night hungry and ate something with too much sugar in it that triggered an allergic reaction to a medical condition he had. His aunt and uncle, Kathy and David Mitchell, said they believe their nephew, who was retarded, tried unsuccessfully to bath himself like he was taught to do in retarded school and accidently drowned. They came to the conclusion that he slipped and knocked himself out by hitting his head on the edge of the tub." Aaron McCalister was the lead detective of the case and Ferguson's boss. He listened to Ferguson, seemingly discerned, but was actually concentrating on every detail. Leaning back in his black leather chair with the palms of his hands pressed against the back of his head and his legs crossed and the heels of his booths resting on top of his oak wood desk, he asked Ferguson, "Who found the boy?"

"The report said his uncle did, when he got up to take a late night piss."

"What about the autopsy report?"

"It hasn't come in yet."

"OK. While we're waiting on that, drive over to the retarded school that the boy went to and find out as much as you can about his medical problem and the training he received at the school to deal with it." Then he adjusted, placing his hands on the armrests of his chair as he said, "And I'll see if I can contact his aunt and uncle at home and get some background information on them." Bryant nodded his head in agreement and folded the report folder together. Leaving it on the desk as he stood up. Then walked out, quietly closing the door behind himself.

McCalister didn't have any problem getting in touch with the Mitchells and them agreeing to talk with him. They lived on the south end of Seattle. So from the station downtown he took Denny and got on I-5 to the Martin Luther King Way exit. Made the loop and took Orthello across Rainier past the Safeway grocery store towards Lake Washington and pulled into the low income Rainier Beach Housing Development. Checking the address numbers as he drove slowly, until he located the right parking lot to pull into. He gave three knocks on the door, heard footsteps, then the door unlocking. And he saw it open by a tall medium built man. "Hello. I'm Lieutenant Aaron McCalister, here to speak with Mr. and Mrs. David and Kathy Mitchell."

It was David Mitchell who answered the door and invited McCalister in. As the two men entered the living room Kathy stood up and was introduced by her husband to the lieutenant. Then David gestured for him to seat himself in one of the cushioned chairs facing the sofa that he and his wife sat down on. "Thank you," McCalister responded. "You're welcome lieutenant. Now, what is it that you'd like for us to tell you?," David inquired. "Well, let me first explain that it's routine procedure for us to get some background information, as much as we can, so that our investigations in matters like this are complete," McCalister told David. "I see. OK. What would you like to know about us?," he asked.

"Let's start with you telling me about yourself. What you do for a living. How you met your wife Kathy."

"Well, right now I'm unemployed and have been for some time. Because for the majority of my life I made my living gambling. But got out of that after I met and fell in love with Kathy and she wanted us to settle down. Back in those days I was in the class of gamblers known as 'high rollers.' And I met Kathy on one occasion that I had been invited to a yacht party that Donovan Tripp was throwing in celebration of a casino he was about to open in the Caribbean, and Kathy and her sister Janis were among the entertainers on board."

"I see. Well, if its not too personal, what happened that changed your profession and life-style?"

"Kathy. She wanted to have kids. So I invested in real estate. But unfortunately, made some bad decisions that led to us losing all of our money. To make a long story short."

"I'm sorry to hear that. And about what has happened to, both, your nephew and his mother.

Now concerning her, your sister Mrs. Mitchell, would you tell me a little bit about your relationship with her? Your husband just mentioned that she and yourself were entertainers."

"Yes we were. Our parents were in the hotel casino business for many years and Janis and I got involved while we were in college. We developed our own act then left school after our mother and father hired us to perform it. Janis and I were always close. Having grown up being mistaken for twins a lot. But weren't, because, we were born a year a part. She was the oldest. When my dad sold his club and retired with my mother and they decided to travel Janis and I kept the house and continued to perform our act on the private circuit. Until I met David. And Janis met Yves, a European film maker. She eventually broke up with him and decided to return to the United States. I was here in Seattle with David because he wanted to hook up with some musician friends he has here that promised to help him get into the business as a songwriter. And when Janis didn't make it as a model, she moved from New York here so we could be close. She also wanted to have kids like me but couldn't because Yves had made her have an abortion. And it left her sterile. So she adopted Ken. And was raising him as a single parent."

In the meantime, while McCalister was interviewing the Mitchells, his partner was at the School For Children With Disabilities collecting the information he needed for the investigation.

Dr. Sam Jackson is the psychologist who met with him. After they introduced themselves, Detective Ferguson asked jokingly, "How often do you get mistaken for Samuel L. Jackson?"

"Quite a bit. But just by the name of course," the doctor responded chuckling. "So, what can I help you with today detective?," asked Jackson.

"Well, unfortunately, it concerns the death of a young adolescent boy. Who, from the report on file with the police department, was trained here to deal with a medical problem he had that required him to take baths or showers whenever he consumed too much sugar. I'm here because its alleged that the kid accidently drowned himself."

"I see. Is this for insurance purposes? Or, because there's a wrongful death lawsuit in the makings?"

"No. Neither one. I'm here strictly on police business. As part of the process to determine the facts. To find out the truth. We have no other way of deciding what is, until we've reviewed all of the evidence. And following up on the accuracy of the statements that were given to the reporting officers is the part of that process that I've been assigned to. That's all."

"Alright. The boy you want to know about is Kenneth Watson. Everyone here is familiar with him because his was a one-and-only case. He was diagnosed with two illnesses. One, retardation. And the other, schist. Medically known as metamorphichypertension. What that means in layman's terms is, the abnormal accelerated rate of the body burning sweet calories. Which causes it to overheat and the brain to begin shutting down. If the body can be cooled down in time the affected person remains conscious. But, if not, the person blanks out. In either situation, however, there is little or no recollection by the person of what happened afterwards. What we taught Ken to do is recognize the symptoms and respond prior to reaching the stage of blacking out. Because of the danger involved. A fatal fall, or, as the case may now be, drowning."

"I see. Well, since you trained him here to respond, was there any certificate or award given to him that proved he successfully completed the program that he was in?"

"Yes. Would you like a copy of that, along with our clinical analysis of his ability to care for himself under those circumstances with his disability?"

"Yes, doctor. That information will be very helpful in this investigation. Thank you."

"You're more than welcome. I'll have it done right away for you. Just wait in the receptionist area. And someone will bring it to you."

Part Two of the Investigation

Karen Stone was investigating the deaths of the two women. Janis Watson and Alice Vargas. The official cause of their deaths had not been determined yet, and like her counterparts of the team, McCalister and Ferguson, she was waiting on the autopsy reports to come in. But at the moment, holding a meeting with them discussing the information that she had retrieved from the field. "I found out that the women made an inquiry at the motel office about 11:30 p.m. Saturday concerning the whereabouts of Mrs. Vargas' husband, Larry. The clerk said that he remembered seeing them leave on foot and walk up the street in the direction of the 8-Ball Tavern when they didn't get an answer at his motel room. So I checked with the tavern's owner and got the phone number of the bartender who worked there that night and he recalled both women coming in asking about Mr. Vargas and telling them that he had been in the bar but left with a man who had been sitting at a table with a friend a few hours before her husband walked in. He said that one was tall and the other one short. And that it was the short one he remembers Vargas leaving with. The tall guy left a little bit after that by himself. The bartender said Ms. Watson and Vargas stood in front of the tavern for a few minutes talking then jay walked across Rainier to the liquor store. He never saw them leave the store. But remembers a lot of people left the tavern to go see what had happened down the street not very long from the time he'd last seen the two woman. Which we all know turned out to be Mrs. Vargas' husband Larry laying in the motel parking lot bleeding to death. I'm estimating they left the motel and returned to the home of Ms. Watson between 12:40 and 1:00 a.m. Sunday morning. Then nearly five hours later, were found laying on Ms. Watson's bed with syringes in their arms, after Kathy Mitchell asked the police who were at her house about the drowning of her nephew to investigate whether her sister had gotten into a car accident on her way there after being told what had happened to her son. Traces of blood were found on the soles of both women's shoes and in the car of Ms. Watson. Also, knives were found in their purses that I discovered matched the set in the kitchen butcher's block that had two missing. None of the neighbors say they saw or heard anything unusual. But the reporting officer stated that the front door of the house was ajar," Stone concluded. Then McCalister said, "Well, somebody saw something. I'm sure of that. We just don't know who?, right at the moment. But what puzzles me?, is, you just mentioned that the front door of the house was left partially opened. I think it could be because someone else was there either when they arrived ,or, after they did. Karen I want you to make arrangements with the confidential information unit upstairs to find out if there has been anyone taken into custody looking for a deal claiming to have information. And Bryant, I want you to return to the house and check for signs of a burglary. And bring in anything you think will help put us on the trail of whoever else might have been there."

McCalister in the meantime got with the lab guys who were working on matching up the fingerprints that had been collected. But so far, no one's identity had turned up. And he also found out that at the morgue the bodies of Larry and Alice Vargas were still waiting to be positively identified by a member of their families before an autopsy on them was performed.

Chapter Eight
Getting the Bad News

The next morning McCalister walked into his office and found a note on his desk that had been left by his superior Captain Frank Phillips. Ordering him to notify members of Larry and Alice Varga's families about their deaths. So the first thing on his agenda when he met with Ferguson and Stone was assigning them the task of getting in touch with the relatives. Not necessary in the case of Janis and Kenneth Watson because Kathy had already contacted her parents about them.

When Kathy's e-mail hit the desktop computer inside their RV Harry and Ginger were enjoying themselves riding on the roller coaster at Disney Land in Anaheim, California. Only if they had cared to turn on their cell phones after getting out of bed that Sunday morning from spending a wonderful night humping on each other, would the fun they were having been erased by the weeping voice messages that Kathy had left for them about Janis and Ken. That they were both dead. Laying in the city morgue waiting for their brains, guts, and blood to be examined.

It was around one o'clock in the afternoon when Allen and Doris Pearson were notified by their answering service to return an important phone call to the Seattle Police Department concerning their daughter Alice. At the time they both were outside helping their workers to inspect the trees of their Florida orange groves. After being made aware of that Allen folded his Motorola together and tossed it onto the dashboard of his SUV and shouted out a quick set of instructions to his work crew's lead man then located his wife and told her they had to get home right away. As he sped down the dirt road leaving a smokey trail of dust swirling in the air he and Doris worried in their conversation that Alice had gotten into some kind of trouble connected with Larry selling marijuana and cocaine again. Or, that she may have gotten into a bad argument with him that led to her being charged with assault, or yet, even worse, manslaughter again. Allen was thinking like that as he reflected on the reason why Alice hadn't finished college. Then he said, "Dam! I hope she's not in trouble again for working as a stripper. Behind some crazy lunatic like that guy was she had to shoot and kill and go to prison behind." He held the corners of his mouth turned down as he waited for Doris to respond. And it only took a second for her to answer, "I think that she buried that lifestyle in her past when she spent those five years locked up and became a Christian." Allen snapped, "That's bullshit! And you know it!" As he drove with a far away look in his eyes. Knowing the that he and his wife were in for hearing some real bad news from the Seattle police department about their delinquent daughter.

In Tijuana, Mexico Floratine Vargas was giving a tea party in her gazebo that stood near the large fish pond where the lawn of her flower garden met with the cactus and avocado trees that helped to shade a portion of she and her husband Richard's spacious property. So it was her maid Bonita that lifted the phone off of the wall mount in the kitchen and answered, "Buenas diaz. La residente Vargas." The caller was a Spanish interpreter from the Seattle Police Department that only revealed to her it was urgent that Mr. and Mrs. Vargas return the important call.

After Bonita had taken the message she hurried out of the kitchen's side door running towards the gazebo shouting, "Senora Vargas! Ahi ah llama emergency para ti!" Bonita's approach silenced the women as they all turned and looked in her direction. Immediately Floratine said, "Permita me porvavor." Then rose from her chair and went to meet her maid a good distance away from her guests. After she heard what Bonita had to tell her Floratine walked briskly back to the foot of the gazebo steps and apologized to her company for having to leave them unexpectedly and said that her maid would help to see them out when they finished. Then she turned and hastened toward her house and called her husband Richard as soon as she got inside.

He was sitting in the office of his lucrative auto paint and upholstery shop reviewing receipts when Floratine got a hold of him. But she was so tearful as she spoke in Spanish over the phone that Richard could hardly make out what she was saying. "Floratine, habla en englis," he politely ordered her. Then in between her sniffles and sobs she said, "A terrible thing has happened to our son."

"What?"

"He's been murdered."

As he listened to his wife burst into a woe so pitiful that she could no longer hold the telephone his mouth hung open in shock as the light in the room faded to black and every sound inside of it faded to silence. He regained all of his senses after a few seconds, wondering by who? And for what reason?, had his only son been killed. Then, unable to get anything else out of his wife, he left the busy shop in the hands of his assistant managers Felix and Pedro. Driving his Porsche 911 fast and erratically through traffic in order to get home as quick as he could.

Chapter Nine
By Any Means Necessary

Ruby Carson was sitting in the King County Jail without bail on a cocaine sales charge, waiting on a parole violation hearing. She knew there was no way out of returning to the women's state prison in Purdy, Washington unless she could get the charge against her dropped and the parole violation hold lifted. Her brain was working overtime trying to figure out who had given that undercover cop Darlene's name as a reference to buy coke from her?, when a female guard walked by and saw her laying on her bunk meditating. "Carson, are you aware that your name was called in the day room?," Officer Gloria Finch asked her standing on the other side of the cell door bars. "No. What for?," Ruby inquired raising up into a sitting position to face Finch. "All I can tell you is Detective Stone is conducting interviews to screen people for possible release. It might be due to overcrowding. Do you want me to have your name put back on the list?"

"Uh– sure. Yeah. Get me back on it. Will she call me out again today?"

"I can check on it for you."

"Thanks. I really appreciate that."

"OK. No problem."

Ruby's mind began to race with so much hope that she couldn't continue to sit. She had to get on her feet and pace the length of the small 6X12 foot cell. Whispering under her breath, "Tell that bitch whatever she wants to hear. Whatever she wants to know... Fuck it. You gotta do what you gotta do..."

Stone stayed late to finish the questioning so that in the morning she could start fresh dealing with the next step of the investigation. And got around to Ruby very close to her lockup time. By morning, Ruby had become even more on edge from not knowing whether the information she had given Stone would get her back on the street. The uncertainty made her lose her appetite for breakfast. So she went back to her cell. And with no one there to see her do it, got on her knees and prayed.

It was Wednesday morning. A little after 9:00 a.m. when McCalister, Ferguson, and Stone began their day by picking up where they had left off at. They were in the conference room as usual, sipping hot Styrofoam cups of coffee. "Karen, did you come up with any leads yesterday," McCalister asked her. "Yes," she answered. "I spoke with a girl name Ruby Carson who's upstairs waiting to be arraigned on a sales charge and can't get out on bail because there's a parole hold on her. She said she doesn't know anything about the murders, but that, there was someone who tried to sell her some credit cards in exchange for coke on the same night that the murders occurred. Who the person was she doesn't know. Only the individual who brought them to her apartment. But she's sure that she can find that information out for me if she were out there on the street. I told her that I'd think about it." Obviously, the big question in Stone's mind was did they really need that information? And to answer it, after a moment of silence Ferguson said, "Well, having that information is important enough for us to have the charges against her dropped since this is a murder investigation. Especially since, the fingerprints found in the home of Janis Watson could match the person's prints who tried to sell Carson the credit card." Then McCalister responded, "See what you can do for her Karen. Talk to the deputy prosecutor downstairs about having the charge dropped and see if her parole officer will cooperate with us to at least have the parole hold temporarily suspended pending the results we get out of her. We need to locate whoever tried to sell her that credit card before they disappear. Immediately Stone responded, "Alright. I'm on it," as she slid back from the table and headed for the door.

Lisa Robinson was the deputy prosecutor who Stone had to get together with about dropping the cocaine sales charge against Ruby. Not possible to do at the time when she left the conference room upstairs because Robinson was in court. So all Karen could do was have the bailiff give Lisa a message to call her at her extension number during recess.

When she got back to her office she had better luck with Ruby's probation officer Joyce Turner. Because she was doing nothing more than taking a few random urine samples for drug testing when Karen called. After she found that out Karen got over to the Smith Tower Building before Robinson had time to finish what she was doing and decide that getting out into the field would be a good way to keep from getting bored. After she explained the reason why she wanted Ruby out of jail, Turner explained to Stone that she'd have to make a call to headquarters to get that type of a request approved. "I don't have the authority to do that. All I can, is, make that recommendation and submit the paperwork. Which will be (1) A contract of Ruby's release conditions and (2) An affidavit stating the police department no longer believes it has probable cause to charge her with the possession and sale of cocaine. I'll work on getting the first thing done. And if you can get the second one did and over to me by one o'clock it's possible we can have an answer from Olympia by 3:00 or 4:00 p.m.," she said. Karen thanked her and left smiling, in a hurry to catch up with deputy prosecutor Robinson and detective Irene Smith.

As the end of another uncertain day neared its conclusion, remarkably, Ruby found herself back inside of the interrogation room. Not only with detective Stone. But this time, also with, deputy prosecutor Lisa Robinson and her parole officer Joyce Turner. While Robinson and Turner stood near the door against the wall behind Stone, she sat at the table facing Ruby. Who had been brought in by a stocky built female jail guard that was standing next to her while she sat with her wrists cuffed resting comfortably in her lap. "OK Ruby. Here's the deal," Stone began. "In exchange for your help in this murder investigation the prosecutor is willing to drop the sales and possession charge pending further investigation. And your parole officer is willing to have your parole hold removed pending the outcome of the lab tests done on the substance you sold to detective Irene Smith. Ms. Turner has told me that she doesn't want to see you lose your job and apartment unless its for something more serious than simple possession of an unknown substance. So if you agree to cooperate with me you'll be released today. Do you understand?"

"Yes."

"Alright. Here's what I want you to do..."

It wasn't until after the dinner meal inside the jail had been served, but finally, Ruby was released. And got to her apartment a little after six o'clock and headed straight for the shower. The shower not only cleaned her body it also relaxed her mind. Helping her to absorb the reality of being out of jail and sitting at her dressing table applying her makeup, getting ready to get dressed and back out on the street. Then just as she began to put on a few pieces of jewelry her phone rang. "Hello."

"Hello. Ruby?"

"Darlene?"

"Yeah girl, it's me. I've been calling your number off and on every since I found out that you were going to be released. I was about to try and get some money put on your books today. What's happening? At first they said that you had a parole violation hold on you. How did you get out?"

"Just lucky. The lab tests on the dope came back negative. Evidently, my money and package got mixed up with somebody else's who had some bunk shit. So my parole officer squashed the parole hold she had on me. But I had to beg her to do it so I wouldn't lose my job and apartment. As a matter of fact, I'm getting dressed to go to work right now."

"Girl, you right, you was lucky. I'm glad you out though. That's for sure."

"Me too. Say, you seen Tina? I need to catch up with that dope fiend bitch about something."

"Dam. You lucky again. She's here at Vivian's. Hold on. I'll put her on the phone. Tina! Telephone! It's Ruby! She wants to talk to you! She just got out! Come to the phone!"

When Tina came to the phone and spoke to Ruby she was promised by her a nice package of good dope if she helped Ruby to catch up with the person that she had brought to her apartment who wanted to trade her some credit cards for coke. "Why? What's up?," she asked. Which forced Ruby to think fast. "I just got cut loose and found out that my apartment has been broken into and all of my clothes, except a few things, were stolen. And I'm wondering if they have any more cards and want to make a deal?"

"I think that it was just a one time thing? I can check it out to be sure, but I need transportation. Can you pick me up?"

"Yeah. Give me about thirty minutes. And tell Darlene I said to hang tight until I get there."

"OK."

It was about 7:30 when Ruby and Tina left Vivian's apartment. Kind of early to be going to the gambling house on 19th and Spruce Street. But luckily, not too early. Ruby waited parked down the street and around the corner from the place in her 1987 canary yellow El Dorado. About twenty minutes later Tina reappeared walking around the corner. Whomp!, went the car door when she shut it. "She hasn't been there in awhile. The only other place that they know of where she normally would be at is the La Villa down on Rainier. But that place has been dead ever since that dude got murdered there by the Asian mafia. At least, that's what I just heard."

"Dam. That's some heavy shit. I must have been in jail when that happened. Well, I'll get you high just for trying to help me get hooked up. Alright?"

"Yeah, that's cool. But where at? Right here in the car?"

"No. I'll take you back to Vivian's if you want me to."

"Uh, uh. There's too many people there who I owe a hit to."

Since Ruby didn't have to be at the Double Tree Inn until ten o'clock and work the desk from then until six in the morning there was plenty of time for her to hang out with Tina and find out whatever else she could. After work she decided it wouldn't hurt to drive by the La Villa. And popped "The Best of Sade" into her cassette player and relaxed driving in the early morning traffic with a few snorts of coke up her nostrils.

By the time she made it to the stoplight on Rainier and McCullen it was a quarter to seven and nobody was lingering in front of the motel. She switched the tape to "Salt and Pepper" and when the light changed she drove past the motel then made a right turn onto the side street and another one to approach the motel on the backside. Slowing to a creep letting down the passenger's window as a guy approached and bent forward to look in and make eye contact with her. "What's up?

You looking for fast or slow? I got em both," he said in a hurry. Get in," Ruby told him. After he closed the door she pulled into an empty stall but kept the car running and said, "Look. I might make a deal with you on something, but it has to be later. Because right now I'm just looking for somebody."

"Who?"

"An Asian chick name Susan. Do you know her?"

"No. But the only Asian broad that I've ever seen around here is the one with Big Money. I think her name might have been Susan? But I don't know."

"Do you have any idea when they might come through here again?"

"No. That could be anytime. Or, maybe never. Dude is from Portland. Shit can happen. Like it did here over the weekend. That's all I can tell you."

"Alright."

After Ruby got home she waited until nine o'clock rolled around then called in and reported everything she had found out to Stone.

Chapter Ten

*W*hen Stone had left the conference room to work on getting Ruby out Ferguson told his boss that yesterday he'd gone back to Janis' house and checked for broken windows, pry marks, and footprints around the building but found nothing. However, inside the house it appeared that someone had taken a lot of her jewelry because the drawers of the box she kept it in were practically empty. He also told McCalister that he'd found a fairly large metal security box that he believes may have served Janis as a safe and contain most of her important records. But the receipts for her ordinary household expenses seemed to all be in a shoebox he found on the shelf in the closet of her bedroom. And said that after he left the house he drove over to the Vargas residence and conducted the same type of search there for telephone and credit card records. Then he commented to McCalister, "You were right."

"About having Carson cut loose?"

"That. And the fact that there aren't any credit cards reported stolen over the weekend. I checked on it."

"So that means, the person who tried selling those cards to Carson is one of our prime suspects."

"Exactly."

From that point forward Ferguson went about the business of collecting more information and found out that Alice Vargas' credit card had been used Sunday morning to purchase some men's and women's clothing at Norstroms downtown and at the Southcenter Mall. And that, Janis Watson's card had been used at the same stores on Sunday around 10:00 a.m. The bank manager at Sea First told him that around 6:00 p.m., as late as yesterday, someone had attempted to use her card again to extract cash from one of the ATMs and the machine ate the card. He estimated between the two banks, Sea First and Washington Mutual, close to a thousand dollars in merchandise was stolen from Norstroms and the Bon Marche' using their cards. The bank and store managers said they would work on getting Ferguson a copy of the video tapes as soon as possible.

After doing all the leg work it took to find out everything that he had Ferguson rested his tired feet, but kept sitting at his desk trying to learn what he could about the times and places that calls had been made to and from the two women's home and cell phones on the day of their deaths. Using the records he found in their homes showing the companies who had provided them with those services.

While Ferguson was gathering the telephone and credit card evidence McCalister spent time examining the photographs taken of Janis and Alice at the crime scene and discovered that neither of them had on any jewelry. So he drove to their homes also and collected whatever photographs he could find of them wearing some. When he returned to the police station he had enlarged copies made of the pictures, focusing on just the jewelry itself. Then made a list of all the fax numbers to the local pawn shops and sent them the pictures with notification that the property had been stolen, asking the shop owners to be on the alert for anyone trying to do business with them for any of it.

The last thing on his list of things to do was getting court authorization for a locksmith to open the metal container belonging to Janis. He wanted to spare the property of being damaged to be opened without a key but couldn't after finding out that Kathy didn't know anything about the box nor where an extra key to it might be.

In the meantime. All of the parents of the decease victims were converging on Seattle. And by the end of the day had found locations to stay at, and had gotten in touch with the police department to announce their arrival and make arrangements to view the lifeless bodies of their loved ones.

For McCalister, Ferguson, and Stone it was never easy standing next to the family members who were obligated to make a positive identification of someone dear to them, when the coroner pulled back the sheet covering the face of the corpse because there were risks involved. At the least could be something as mild as the smell of shit coming from someone's underpants who lost control of that bodily function at the grisly sight revealed to them. And at the worst could be something as violent as getting blamed as a police officer and attacked for not preventing what had happened from happening. But none of that took place this time. Only sad faces, tears, and when it came to Larry's mother, "Oh mi Dios!," when she saw the large stitched up Frankenstein looking gash on the side of her dead son's neck.

Chapter Eleven
Bruce Biggs

Bruce Biggs was a life insurance policy investigator for Pacific Atlantic. A company paid by a group of life insurers to settle claims of their policy holders. His office was located in the Traveler's Insurance Company Building downtown Seattle on Denny next to the Interstate-5 freeway overpass.

His caseload was heavy. And it had been a long time since he'd settled a claim with the man he saw on the Sunday evening news on channel 8. So it wasn't until an entire week later, after he hung up the phone explaining to Kathy that she could come in and pick up a partial payment check that would cover the funeral expenses of her sister and nephew, that the name Mitchell rung a bell. He rose and took a few steps over to his file cabinet and searched until he found the folder he was looking for then sat down in his swivel rocker high back office chair thumbing through it and discovered that his hunch was right, he had just spoken to David Mitchell's wife on the telephone. There was no time to waste he thought. And got on the phone again. "City of Seattle Police Department. Sergeant Mills speaking. How can I help you," he asked his unknown caller. "Yes. I'm an investigator with the Pacific Atlantic Life Insurance claims department and would like to speak with the person in charge of investigating the recent deaths of a woman by the name of Janis Watson and her son Kenneth Watson. I have some very important information about the husband of the deceased woman's sister. I'm handling her life insurance policy settlement and believe what I know about her husband could be helpful," Biggs relayed in an urgent tone of voice. "OK. Hold on. I'll transfer you," Mills quickly responded.

When Lieutenant McCalister took the call from Biggs he had just returned from lunch and was reaching for the stack of folders he saw in the 'incoming' mail bin that sat on the corner edge of his desk. They were the autopsy reports he found out as he listened with the telephone receiver held to his ear using the side of his face and shoulder. When Biggs finished McCalister agreed with him that they should meet and asked him to come in.

By doing some fast walking and catching one of the free-zone buses, Biggs arrived very quickly and was led to the conference room where McCalister and the rest of his investigation team were waiting. After being introduced and shaking hands McCalister sat down next to Stone ready to hear what Biggs had to offer. He himself, who was seated next to Ferguson on the opposite side of the large table, began by saying, "Well, to begin with, David Mitchell is part of an ongoing F.B.I. criminal investigation that has many aspects to it. Illegal distribution and sales of weapons and drugs, promotion of slavery for prostitution—foreign and domestic, and car insurance fraud scams. Which is how I became involved with him. I've had to settle several accident injury claims with attorneys he'd hired to collect substantial amounts of money on his behalf from the company I work for.

****

David grew up in Long Beach, California. His father was a navy man stationed there at the base. But unfortunately died in the Viet Nam war when the call to duty came. The loss devastated his mother. And she became an alcoholic. Which in turn, had a dramatic psychological affect on David that only seem to worsen the more his mother drank. David fought a lot at school but it wasn't until he got into trouble for robbery using a gun that he'd stolen in a burglary that he developed an arrest record. Which ironically helped his mother because the court ordered her to attend counseling sessions with him at the California Youth Authority Center where he was ordered taken into custody.

During that time David's mother Francis got a waitress job and met a man name Slim Shaky. A well known gambler who associated very closely with players and pimps. Eventually, Slim and David's mother began to have a steady relationship. And at some point he showed David how he made his money was by playing poker. And taught him the game. For a while they played as a team in after hour gambling houses in a number of different states. Showing up separately at different times. Winning more than losing. Then Slim went to New York to hang out with some friends and attend the big Allen vs. Foster event. The one that Style Magazine covered and took pictures of the 'super fly' crowd that came for the showdown in carriages, Rolls Royces, and Bentleys. Wearing all kinds of expensive tailor made clothes and flashy custom made jewelry. Unfortunately, with the help of local jealous undercover cops who used the magazine photographs as justification to launch an income tax investigation, many of them were busted by the IRS after all the hoopla. Which luckily, Slim didn't get caught up in.

At the fight, and purely by coincidence, he got seated next to a stock exchange broker named Mary Wilson. They ended up getting acquainted with each other by casually exchanging comments about the fight in between rounds. But even better acquainted after making a bet with each other on who would win. When Slim's fighter came out on top Mary stayed true to her word and paid up by playing strip poker in her Manhattan Townhouse with him, until, both of them were butt ass naked. Slim had her after that. Later on into their relationship is when he found out that she had investments on the N.Y. Stock Exchange and he got interested in how it operates. And she used one word to describe it to him. "Trends." And told him that being good at predicting them is what makes people successful at making money in that business. And the intrigue of being able to do that himself, and of course, the good sex that Mary was laying on him, were two good reasons for him to stay in New York. But of course, not forever. Just long enough to master a different kind of poker game.

Back in sunny California David had gotten good enough playing poker to strike out on his own. And whenever he sat down at a table in a gambling house or Indian reservation casino, he usually won more than he lost, using the skills that Slim taught him. He kept stacking his money like he had learned to do. And eventually graduated to the status of being a high roller in Las Vegas, Caribbean Islands, and Rio De Janeiro. Literally, going from rags to riches overnight. Next, David aspired into the Asian culture during that time by finessing Li Chang into his bed. As co-owner and CEO of Magnet Enterprises she was considered to be a whale at the Tripp Hotel and Casino in Las Vegas, Nevada. A filthy rich Chinese electronics manufacture of high speed computer chips.

He spotted her having fun but losing badly at her dice table. "She's beautiful isn't she. And unattached from what I hear," Lomax Flowers, the hotel manager mentioned to David as they stood next to each other observing from a moderate distance. It hadn't been too long ago that Lomax had registered David as a high roller at the casino and they'd become friends. "Well, if she's not attached, who's the guy with her?, David asked.

"I'm pretty sure it's one of her body guards and not her boyfriend, if that's what you're thinking."

"How did you guess that I wonder?"

"Rudimentary. I knew you would never have asked me that question if you weren't suspecting that he might be someone like that. In spite of, all of my intellectual insights and mystical powers to know that he isn't."

"In that case, I'm about to find out if her preference is tall, dark, and handsome."

"And specifically, you of course."

"Absolutely. Without a doubt."

"Well, how do you propose to do that when she's at a reserved private table? And not only her bodyguard, but house security as well, is going to stop you as soon as you get too close?"

"Elementary. Just become invisible. Then walk right up and whisper something in her ear that she wants to hear."

"If you can do that, I'll introduce you to Mr. Tripp. The billionaire himself. But better yet, all you have to do is just, 'fade out' a little bit. Ha, ha, ha, ha... And I'll make sure you get on the list as a guest to one of his yacht parties. Ha, ha, ha."

"Is that a deal?"

"That's a deal. You have my word on it."

"Alright. Stay right here–til you see me reappear."

Lomax was laughing under his breath like Johnny Carson as he watched David turn and walk out of sight into the lounge. Shortly after he seated himself a waitress was at his table leaning forward listening carefully. When he finished explaining his plan she walked away and returned with an ink pen and clear white napkin. And he wrote, "Words of encouragement," on the outside flap and sketched and jotted something on the inside folds of it. "Thirty of that is a tip and the other twenty is to put a rush on getting it delivered with a tray of iced oriental tea," David told the waitress as he handed her a fifty dollar bill. When he stood up, he walked over to the bar counter and saw Lomax gazing his head around and glancing at his wrist watch. Then as he walked out of the shadows of the lounge entrance to resume his former position next to his friend he saw a bellhop pushing a cart with the tray of iced tea and small stack of napkins on it over to the filthy rich Chinese woman's private table. It distracted her dice tossing frenzy, but pleasantly, it appeared to everyone who noticed.

As instructed, the bellhop raised the top napkin to expose the one underneath it to her. In a way that, no one except her could see. Then he politely gestured with his hand that no tip was necessary and walked away. She took a few more rolls trying to make her number, but didn't. After that she stopped. And took several of the napkins off the stack and walked towards the lounge. Leaving David and Lomax both in suspense. Lomax, about whether the hotel was about to lose an invaluable customer behind his bull shitting around with David? And David, about that too, plus, the consequences to himself in the realm of high rollers? To everyone else on the gambling floor there didn't seem to be anything out of the ordinary happening. So both men remained poised. Smiling and observing the action. But on the inside, they were nervous as hell.

Her bodyguard lingered close by waiting for her to come out of the ladies room. When she did, he noticed that she had disposed of the napkins. Completely unaware it was only after reading David's message several times staring at the sketch he drew depicting his hard black dick and dangling balls. Visualizing before she came out of the stall what it would feel like for him to... and her to...

After she got back to her table she really didn't believe that his advice would help her to win anything, but just for the hell of it, had her bodyguard fix a cup of the tea then took a sip of it, and placed a double or nothing bet on the dice. Then picked them up, shook and blew, then slung them to the embankment wall and watched the numbers three and four turn up. "Lucky seven! You're a winner!," the dice raker called out. Drawing the attention of the small gathering of onlookers and other players at private tables. They cheered and clapped to her change of luck, encouraging her to roll the dice again. It was then, with the shift in peoples' movement, that Li made eye contact with David for the first time. And was impressed by how tall, handsome, and well dressed he was. "I think she's looking at you David," Lomax said under his breath. "She is," he replied in the same manner nodding his head with a gentlemen's smile on his face. Li took that as a go-ahead from him to bet and roll the dice again. But it hadn't been. And as soon as he saw her pick them up to roll he realized his mistake, but had no way to turn back the hands of time and correct it. His mind was to walk away and avoid being any part of the woman's embarrassment when she lost her winnings back to the casino. But his poker instinct overrode that impulse and he stayed and called the poker hand that fate was holding. Then heard, "Lucky seven again! You're a winner!" Then David said, "That's my go Joe. Sorry. But, I gotta blow."

When Li saw David making his exit she stopped gambling. And dismissed her bodyguard from duty, on her way to the elevator. Then secretly rendezvoused with David in his suite...

Lomax had to wait a while to make good on the deal he made with David because Li Chang took him to China with her. It was an unusual arrangement. But the Chinese government didn't squawk because Magnet Enterprises was one of the nation's biggest companies and financial contributors to its military.

David continued to gamble in Asia until his luck changed. And it was unfortunate for him that in the process of trying to regain it he accumulated huge debts. The casinos took his word that he would pay what he owed them because they thought Li Chang was backing him. But found out, that in spite she was otherwise taking care of David, he had continued to be his own man. When she learned of his debts she wanted to pay them off but couldn't because David owed Satan himself. The only alternative she had to help him was sneak safely out of Asia back into the United States. Then wire him enough cash to sustain himself for a while. The F.B.I. learned from the IRS it was several million. Which didn't last him very long. Because the people he owed in China got in touch with their mafia connections in the U.S. With instructions to kill David if he didn't immediately cough up a substantial part of his debt.

****

The background that Biggs gave on David Mitchell was full of intrigue and incredible to say the least. "How much does he owe the mafia?," McCalister asked Biggs. "According to the F.B.I. field agent that I'm in contact with it's still in the millions. My guess is, it equals the three million dollar life insurance policy pay-out that I've just spoken to his wife about," Biggs said. "And why do you think that?," Stone intervened. "Because, I think, when his debt was much larger than that it never occurred to him the insurance policy his wife's sister had on her son and herself could be of any help to solve his life threatening financial problem. But now that his debt is down to the same amount as the insurance pay-out, you see." Ferguson picked it up from there and said, "Which explains the reason for the long delay." And Biggs responded, "That's right."

"Ok. We'll consider the Mitchells as suspects, but we can't charge them with anything until we have proof they're responsible for the deaths of Janis Watson and her adopted son. In the meantime, I would appreciate it Mr. Biggs if you contacted me again as soon as you're able to get more information from your F.B.I. friend," McCalister said. Finalizing the meeting.

Although Biggs had a good theory, it still didn't seem possible to McCalister that David had somehow managed to convince his wife to help kill her sister and nephew just to clear up his overseas gambling debts. Unless, not only was there a serious threat on his life, but hers as well. Or, perhaps their children or parents maybe? Clearly though, one way or the other, after listening to Biggs there was a lot more to solving this case than he had imagined.

Chapter Twelve
The Grand Jury's Secret Indictments

*T*he closed hearing was being held in the courtroom of the Honorable Judge Julius Tanner. He was presiding over the proceedings of the grand jury for the purpose of determining whether the evidence accumulated by detectives McCalister, Ferguson, and Stone was strong enough for there to be charges filed and an arrest made concerning the deaths of Kenny Watson, Janis Watson, Alice Vargas, and Larry Vargas. When the judge entered the court room everyone stood then sat. Shortly after his introduction and giving an explanation for the presence of the grand jury, he instructed King County's lead prosecutor Darrell Epson to call his first witness. "I'd like to call Detective Karen Stone of the Seattle Police Department, your honor." Then Tanner said, "Will detective Karen Stone please step forward." After she was sworn in by the bailiff and seated Epson proceeded to ask his first question. "Detective Stone would you please explain to the grand jury how you became involved in this case?"

"Yes. On the night of April 1, 1996 four deaths occurred in Seattle that involved a retarded minor named Kenneth Watson, his mother Janis Watson, her friend Alice Vargas, and her husband Larry Vargas. Myself and two other detectives of the police department, Lieutenant Aaron McCalister and Sergeant Bryant Ferguson, were assigned to investigate them."

"Alright. Beginning with the minor, explain the cause of his death, and then, that of the other three victims."

"Kenneth Watson died from strangulation. His mother Janis Watson died from a drug overdose, as well as her friend Alice Vargas. And Alice's husband, Larry Vargas, died by bleeding to death from a sever slash on the left side of his neck and a puncture wound to his upper abdomen."

"And how can you be sure that each death was caused by what you just testified to they were?"

"By relying on the autopsy report of each victim that the city of Seattle's medical examiner provided the police department with."

"Thank you. Your honor that's all for this witness."

Ferguson took the stand next. "Detective, according to what your fellow investigator just testified, the deaths of Kenneth Watson and Larry Vargas weren't accidental. But, the deaths of Alice Vargas and Janis Watson who both died from drug overdose, could have been. Is there any reason for you to think otherwise? And if so, who do you think is responsible for these deaths?"

"First, we have probable cause to believe David Mitchell and his wife Kathy are responsible for the death of Kenneth Watson because they wanted to deprive the boy of his two million dollar inheritance he was entitled to for being the primary beneficiary of that amount in case of his mother's accidental death. And secondly, we possess evidence that proves, even though Alice Vargas and Janis Watson are now dead, they plotted and successfully killed Larry Vargas for having a sexual encounter with Ms. Watson's retarded son Kenny. And perhaps to eliminate his possible discovery and interference with an affair that Janis' diary gives details of."

"I see. Thank you detective. Your honor, I'd like to call Lieutenant Aaron McCalister as my next and final witness."

"Alright. Mr. Ferguson, step down. And Mr. McCalister, you step forward."

After McCalister exchanged places with Ferguson on the witness stand he testified that a certified copy of life insurance investigator Bruce Biggs' report concerning Kathy Mitchell's entitlement to a three million dollar payment for the untimely deaths of her sister and nephew proved that she and her husband had motive to kill their retarded nephew because of the life threatening indebtedness he was in to the Asian mafia.

Information that was supplied to Biggs by confidential F.B.I. sources. Additionally, he told the grand jury that the Mitchells had lied about their nephew drowning because the official autopsy report proved he died from being choked to death. He stated also that a metal security box belonging to Janis Watson was found at her home and contained, among other personal effects, a diary that described what had sexually taken place between her son and Larry Vargas and what she and his wife felt about it and the course of action they decided to take. He also mentioned that DNA testing proved that Larry's blood was found to be identical to the blood found on the soles of both women's shoes. And that, knives were found inside of their purses with blades consistent with inflicting the deep cut on Larry's neck and stab to his abdomen. Lastly, he testified that David's fingerprints had been found on the doorbell button of Janis' house. And on the outside and inside of the front door. And on the handle of her upstairs bedroom home telephone. And that, the last two calls made from the phone were to the home of his mother and step-father, and his own residence using its 3-way calling feature.

By the hearing's end the grand jury concluded that very likely the person using the alias Big Money was David Mitchell based on his former high roller reputation and past relationship with Li Chang. Also, if true that the F.B.I. links him to an Asian drug distribution ring, what Ruby Carson testified to about an Asian woman name Susan having had the stolen credit cards and sells heroin was circumstantial enough to prove David was at the motel with her and spotted Alice and Janis making their get-away after killing Larry. Which convinced the jurors that Epson had a good case.

Not On My Watch

After the grand jury adjourned it was normal practice for judge Tanner to review evidence, if time and circumstances permitted. He was diligent in that regard because he aspired to be appointed a position on the court of appeals. And therefore, made every attempt to catch any appealable error he may have committed during a proceeding before it reached the point of being too late to voluntarily correct himself. It just so happened that he did have time to do it after the hearing that day, so he disrobed inside his chambers and poured a glass of brandy to help himself relax while he looked the case over.

He started with Kenny Watson's folder. Because he wanted to know whether there had been some legitimate reason for the Mitchells to have told police they believed he had accidently drowned. And right away, Tanner stumbled upon the School For Children With Disabilities' clinical analysis report. And found that Ken's physical reaction to eating too much sugar included having a penis erection. With that information Tanner quickly formed the opinion that something besides collecting the boy's insurance policy money could have been their reason for lying. "Now things are going to get interesting," the judge thought to himself smiling. Celebrating it by taking another sip of brandy...

After reviewing two reports– Tanner made a decision to squash the secret murder indictments against David and Kathy first thing in the morning. And issued four emergency subpoenas ordering Epson, McCalister, Ferguson, and Stone to appear in his courtroom at 9:00 a.m. for a rehearing of the evidence.

The Rehearing

After he succeeded at getting the Mitchells indicted Epson drove his Cadillac Escalade to a parking lot on the pier front beneath I-99, parked, and casually strolled across the trolley car tracks and narrow two lane street that had slow moving traffic. Ironically, Godfathers had a sports bar inside that catered exclusively to the judicial and law enforcement crowd. So it wasn't a surprise to him when he found detectives Ferguson and Stone relaxed having a drink together. "Go Seahawks," they cheered.

McCalister on the other hand drove to the ferry dock and rode the boat over to Mercer Island. On his way, he got out of his Lexus and stood on deck to soak in the smell of crisp air and lake water, the sight of Seattle's shoreline– with the Space Needle in the backdrop, and the screeching sound and sight of the hovering seagulls that were playfully attempting to catch bits of food that were being tossed into the air by many passengers for them to catch and gobble down. When he arrived at home he had nothing on his mind except executing arrest warrants for David and Kathy on murder charges for the strangulation death of their nephew. He forgot it was his birthday and didn't notice that his wife Cynthia had gone out of her way to prepare him a good meal. Over the years she had learned to let her detective husband get whatever it was on his mind off of it first. So she listened. Then surprised him with what he likes most. A blow job. The next day, Ferguson relayed that Judge Tanner had squashed the secret indictments against David and Kathy, and had ordered the three of them and Epson back to his courtroom. "When?," McCalister asked. "Right now," Stone said coming in behind Ferguson and beating him to the punch with the answer.

Since Tanner had squashed the indictments there was no need for the presence of a grand jury. So he held the rehearing of evidence in the confines of his chamber. "Everyone is here judge," his clerk advised him politely peeking in around the door. "OK. Have them come in," he told her. They quietly trailed in and Debbie closed the door behind them. Then Tanner told them to sit down and after they had he said, "You're here because I find fault in the presentation of the evidence that the grand jury was given to consider yesterday. Fault that, had I not discovered it last night, would have tainted my record with a serious appealable error." Epson had an idea what Tanner had discovered but kept quiet. While, McCalister indicated he wanted to comment, but was told by the judge not to interrupt his speech. Then to answer the question he knew that McCalister had, he said, "This is not a fault in any testimony that was given. What it's about, and I think you already know Mr. Epson, is non-disclosure of (1) The clinical analysis report on Kenneth Watson, and (2) The family background report on the Mitchells. After making these two discoveries I simply had no choice but to do what I have. Because David Mitchell, Jr. and his sister Lori are of ages to be just as capable as either one of their parents to have killed Kenneth Watson after finding their six year old brother Perry Mitchell in the same compromising position with Kenny that he was found in with Larry Vargas by his mother and Larry's wife earlier that day. And if either of the teenagers did and killed their cousin, that means, the only reason why David and Kathy lied to the police was to protect their children. And not because they had committed any crime themselves and were attempting to cover it up. So, the indictments against them for murder had to be squashed for the lack of probable cause. Otherwise, they had an appealable fourth amendment violation of the constitution. The type of thing that I can't allow to happen in my courtroom, EVER AGAIN!" That bark from the judge made them flinch. Then happy with that effect, he resumed a normal tone of voice. "And if it ever does Mr. Epson, you're going to find 'yourself' in a hearing, before the American Bar Association for withholding crucial evidence from a grand jury. Is that clear?"

"Yes your honor. I'm very sorry sir. I swear."

"Good. Now, because young Ken was strangled to death you still have a chance to acquire an amended murder indictment. The only thing is, you four have to just figure out against who? And show probable cause. But, nonetheless, don't fret," Tanner dubiously advised. Then explained. "Because you still have murder indictments sitting here on my desk against the two dead women. The most ridiculous thing I ever heard of. But, if you want me to I'll let you go ahead and make an even bigger fool of yourself than you already have," Tanner said with a sigh. And cracked a sly smile when Epson answered, "No sir."

"I was hoping not. Alright. This hearing is over."

The judge had played a game on the detectives and prosecutor about having murder indictments sitting on his desk against Janis and Alice for suspicion of killing Larry. They were really blank affidavit forms he deliberately sat on his desk to have some fun for the sake of being the one who got the last laugh. And laughed the hardiest. After making them regret having tried to get over on him.

Chapter Thirteen

When they walked out of Judge Tanner's chambers none of them said anything until they reached the hallway in front his courtroom. Then McCalister said, "It looks like we're back to square one." They continued down the hall and made the corner to wait on an elevator. And after pressing the button to go down Epson said, "We need to have a meeting. Today if possible. And come up with some type of strategy to get a confession." By the time that they stepped out the elevator a decision had been made by them to meet in the conference room on the second floor that McCalister regularly uses, within the next half hour. Giving themself enough time to do everything they needed to before getting started.

Epson dictated a memo to be posted in the prosecuting attorney's office that explained the current status of the case. Ferguson reported the same thing to the chief of police captain's office. Stone made sure the conference room would be available. And McCalister contacted Bruce Biggs on the phone and told him the disappointing news that no charges could be filed against David and Kathy Mitchell.

After Biggs got the news he had no choice but to authorize a joint-policy three million dollar life insurance payment for the untimely deaths of Janis and Ken. But he wanted to stall as long as he could to see if McCalister would come up with something. So he lied and told Kathy that because of the large sum of money involved it would take a little longer than normal to process the check. "But come in today if you can with a certified copy of the death certificates and sign an affidavit swearing that in no way did you contribute to or cause the deaths of your sister and nephew and that will get the paperwork rolling," he told Kathy.

As soon as she got off the phone Kathy yelled, "We're rich!" Then began to get frisky with David on the living room sofa, where he sat watching Sports Center. But after a few swipes at him with a pillow from the couch she plopped down close to his side and returned to her normal self. Very quickly remembering what she was going to do with the insurance money if everything went as planned. Then cuddling her husband she somberly said, "Well, at least for a minute anyway. But spending it to clear up your debt is worth a lot more than being rich. Because we'll have our lives back. And that's the most important thing in this world to me right now. And will always be." Kissing the side of David's face and hugging him.

"So when do you get the money?"

"Well, I'm not sure exactly. Because he said that it's going to take a little bit longer because of the amount. But he told me if I brought in the death certificates today and signed an affidavit it would start the process."

"OK. And after we take care of that we'll put in our applications for the passports and visas while we're downtown. Go ahead and start getting ready. And I'll catch up after I contact one or two people. You can call Harry and Ginger when we come back. Because we need to get this shit done quick, fast, and in a hurry. Before things change."

"OK."

That was Thursday morning. Four days after Harry and Ginger had left Seattle full of hate and resentment towards their daughter's husband. Not because he was black. But because of what Kathy had already done and was intending to do next for him. First, it was selling the house they'd given their two daughters. And second, if she got it, was going to be using the three million dollars coming from her dead sister and nephew's life insurance policy to finish paying off David's gambling debts. So, laying their beloved oldest daughter and adopted grandson to rest at the Pine Crest Memorial Cemetery was agonizing for Harry and Ginger. And dealing with that situation would not have gone smoothly if Slim Shaky and Francis had not been there in David's support. And Slim giving them some serious chess game lessons.

During that same time Allen and Doris Pearson left Seattle with their beloved daughter's body immediately after making a positive identification of Alice before the autopsy took place. Returning to Florida with it in a refrigerated casket because they wanted her to be buried there in the family's plot at Peaceful Meadows Cemetery. Except, she was being buried much sooner than anyone ever imagined that she would be. During the funeral there were silent tears rolling down the cheeks of those most hurt. And silent memories flowing through the minds of those most endeared by her. Which included, Cee Cee and Blake.

Meanwhile. Larry's parents, Richard and Florantine Vargas, left Seattle in turmoil a week after viewing his body in the crept like atmosphere of the coroner's vault. Because for one thing, Richard had always resented Larry for marrying outside of his race. And for another one, he felt that Larry had disgraced the family's name and reputation again. But even worse, this time, by being caught voluntarily offering his ass to a thirteen year old retarded boy. Florantine was hurt too, but as she always had done, defended her only son. And tried to persuade her husband to fly his body back to Mexico to bury. But Richard was so angry and disgusted that instead of doing that he paid only to have it cremated. Then took a cab back to the cheap motel where Larry had died in a puddle of his own blood and tossed the urn with his ashes in it into the dumpster that sat on the edge of the parking lot.

Chapter Fourteen

David had been right to tell Kathy that they had to get things done quick, fast, and in a hurry. Because just two days later, McCalister and Ferguson were in an unmarked police car on their way to give them a surprise visit.

When the meeting to develop a confession plan ended it had been decided that as much as four arresting officers and a back unit wasn't necessary. Because if the plan failed there wouldn't be any arrest. Besides, the Mitchells were waiting on a three million dollar life insurance policy check so obviously they weren't going to run off and leave it. Since, they had no way of knowing that second-degree murder charges were pending. "Which one do you think did it?," Ferguson asked McCalister as he rode shotgun sipping his lidded cup of coffee bought at the Winchell's on Rainier and Martin Luther King Way. "Well, I'm pretty sure that it's the boy's uncle and not his aunt. But a woman is certainly capable of doing something like that."

"Yeah. Angela Gates and Sandra Smith certainly proved that to be a fact."

Ferguson's mention of those murders silenced the two detectives by the thought of how horrific it was for the children in those cases to have died the way they did. Neither man said another word for a long while as McCalister drove with a determined expression on his face.

David and Kathy were expecting McCalister because he'd given them a courtesy call in advance. Saying that answering just a few more questions would close the case file. This he had done not only to make sure that they were home, but also, to make sure they remained there without suspecting that one or the other was going to be taken into custody for the death of their nephew, if he got the confession that the prosecutor needed.

Ordinarily, McCalister would have taken the freeway in order to save time making the drive. But didn't this time because David said that he and Kathy needed to do some things around the house first. But really, all they wanted to do was have enough time to enjoy fucking each other again. In the morning after their kids had gone to school was always the best time for them. Because then, Kathy could scream and moan like she wanted to and not worry about it.

It was about 11:20 a.m. when David answered the detective's knock on his door and invited them in. And as soon as they were seated he asked, "Now, what else is it that you gentlemen would like to know?" As Kathy sat beside him with a trace of apprehension in the expression she had on her face. Mainly because the detectives had sat on the edge of their seats, as though they were readying themselves for something. Either a quick visit. Or, to take quick action. "Well, first, we'd like to inform you and your wife that it appears your nephew's death wasn't accidental," Ferguson said sternly. "What?!," David responded in an attempt to portray disbelief. "That's right. And lieutenant McCalister and I need you and your wife's cooperation to determine whether it's going to be just one or the both of you that we arrest for the crime."

What Ferguson said made David's mouth drop open and Kathy squirm, letting out a squeaky fart as she did. David sat with a raised set of eyebrows and face rapidly paling while Kathy's face redden with embarrassment and fear. Instinctively, David placed his arm behind her neck and scooted closer. Then McCalister took over and said, "David we have enough evidence to charge both you and your wife with murder, but wanted to spare the two of you the hardship of being arrested for the same crime and having your children taken into custody by the Department of Social and Health Services. Which no doubt will ultimately result with them being placed in separate foster homes. We're aware Kathy that your parents are financially able to care for the children, however, the process involved for them to gain their custody, should they need to, will be a very long and complicated process once DSHS is called upon by the police department to provide care. It's up to the two of you to decide whether they come home from school today with one parent still here. Or, be held at school until they can be picked up and taken into state child care custody. Because, neither of you will be." Kathy responded by placing one hand cupped over her mouth. Then put both hands over her face, lowered her head, and let out sobs of sorrow. While David's reaction was, first, looking up into the void of the ceiling. Then lowering his head with a sigh as he shook it slowly from side to side. McCalister and Ferguson sat quietly for several moments to give them a chance to regain their composure. But were ready to pounce on either one of them if they tried to make a break for it. Finally, David coaxed Kathy to sit up and face the detectives with him. Then he asked, "What about an attorney?" And Ferguson answered, "We'll arrange for you to have one as soon as you get downtown." Then David gave Kathy a hug and whispered in her ear, "It's going to be alright." And lightly kissed the side of her forehead. "OK. I'm ready," he said. Then all three men stood and David positioned himself to be handcuffed.

Once they were at the police station Ferguson and McCalister led David through the underground parking lot security entrance and got buzzed in. Then walked down a spacious well-lit corridor that took them to an elevator. Ferguson pressed the button and the door opened after a short wait. They got off on the second floor and David was taken to a holding cell. Ferguson and McCalister left him there for about ten minutes to turn in their weapons and sign in. Then they returned and read David his Miranda rights. "Well David," McCalister began. "Let me start by telling you what we have that authorizes us to bring murder charges against you. According to the statement you gave police, you were the one who found your nephew, which makes you the most likely person between you and your wife to have had the opportunity to kill him. Now, since we know that certain foods over stimulated him and caused his penis to erect, we believe that you may have discovered the boy doing something totally unacceptable to one of your children when you got up in the middle of the night to take a piss and looked in on them. But we know for a fact that he didn't drown. Not only because we have proof that he was very capable of taking his own baths and showers when he had an allergic reaction to eating too much sugar, but more importantly, because he did not have any water in his lungs according to the autopsy report."

David sat on the small bench inside the holding cell peering into the concrete floor as though he had x-ray vision and was watching the events taking place beneath the depth of it. Silent. Appearing to both detectives to be on the verge of confessing with just a little bit more persuasion that he had no better alternative. So, Ferguson applied more pressure by telling him, "It would behoove you at this point David to admit your guilt because now we can talk to the prosecutor and make a recommendation for a sentence to be imposed on the low end of the scale based on your cooperation with us and not to put the state taxpayers to the unnecessary burden of a lengthy trial. And there are two more pieces of evidence that we have that makes me suggest that. One, is the fact that we have photographs of your nephew's injuries that could only have come from a struggle and not a slip in the tub, and in particular, the one he sustained on the side of his head, we can prove was inflicted after he was dead. And two, is the fact that the prosecutor can amend the charge to include your wife as a co-defendant if you decide to take this to trial. If that happens, there is a very good chance of you both being convicted of murder. Because your debt to the Asian mafia is information that's been shared with us by the F.B.I. That might convince a jury you and your wife had a motive to kill in order to collect insurance policy money to keep the mob from hurting or killing someone close to you if you didn't clear up your debt. Also, we found fingerprints at your sister-in-law's house David that prove you were the last person there after she and her friend died. And have telephone records to substantiate that, plus, prove that before you drove home the purpose of calling your wife may have been to report to her that the deed had been done where you were, and that, you were coming there to do the second one. Either way, it's enough circumstantial evidence to convince a jury that you're guilty of first degree murder." The spastic contortions on David's face revealed the pressure was to great, as he lifted his lowered head and looked pitifully into the eyes of the detectives. Then he broke and said, "It was me." McCalister and Ferguson waited for more.

"I had been out drinking and decided to drop by my sister-in-law's house. And found her and her friend Alice had been partying there doing drugs. And left them sleeping it off. I was pretty tipsy when I let myself out of the house so I drove slow going home. Later on in the night, I got up to take a piss and found the situation that you described. My nephew taking advantage of our six year old. Perry. At least I thought that when I heard, 'let me suck it. Dos this feel good?' And didn't hesitate a second busting into my son's room full of rage and going berserk. My son didn't seem to know why I was yelling and cursing and doing what I was to his cousin. And he scream and cried. All the noise woke up my wife and two older kids. And they ran in and tried to stop me when they saw what was going on. I didn't have any idea that my son had gotten into some poison ivy that evening running after a Frisbee, and that my nephew was sucking on his arm imitating what he'd seen my wife doing to ease the pain. I just imagined the worse when I saw them moving around under the cover on the bed. Once I came to my senses and realized my mistake I panicked. Then dragged him into the bathroom and rammed my his head against the edge of the bath tub. Filled it with water. And placed him in it to make it appear that he had accidently drowned. Then I told my wife to call the police."

After it was clear to the detectives that David had nothing more to say he was removed from the holding cell and booked on second-degree murder charges. But at his arraignment, his public appointed attorney entered a plea of not guilty in his behalf. Not that he thought David was innocent, but because it was standard legal procedure.

Two weeks after David's arrest Judge Tanner walked out of the courthouse on the secluded, sloped, Fourth Street side of the building. Where a small band of cameramen and news reporters were waiting on the steps for him to answer a few questions... "Yes, there's going to be a trial. And no. I will not be presiding," Tanner responded. Then over the gibberish he was asked, "Why not, your honor?" And answered, "Because I presided over the grand jury indictment proceeding and by rule the trial proceeding must go before a different judge." Then he raised both hands and said, "No more questions." His car was in the courthouse garage, so he followed his two-man deputy sheriff escort back into the building and caught the elevator to it.

Chapter Fifteen
Back at the Park Table

Linda had been listening to Al with her undivided attention, in between taking an occasional experimental puff on the marijuana cigarettes that he was smoking. And at this point, asked him, "Where's that paper sack you had?"

"Behind me right here."

"Do you have some more cups in it?"

"Yeah."

"Well, pour me some of that wine in one. This stuff that you got me smoking is making me thirsty."

"Alright."

As he was preparing Linda's drink she took another hit on the joint and passed it back.

In the meantime, the park activities had livened up with a lot more people on and around the basketball court. But Butch was finally bored and hungry. And came out from under the bench and gave Al a bark and stern look to let him know it. So he waved his hand and said, "Go home." Knowing his dog always had a large bowl of dried dog food put out for him by his mother, Ora Wise, on the back porch of the small rented two bedroom house they lived in on 107th Street near the Watts Towers. He and Linda watched his dog trot off. Then Al continued with the rest of the story...

Chapter Sixteen
Five Fingers and Quick Getaway

The white and gold trim Rolls Royce Silver Spur that Slim Shaky drove moved in stealth silence through traffic as he rode on the Hollywood freeway with Francis inside the car with him heading to the L.A. International Airport. He had on his power blue and white trim V-neck silk short sleeve shirt. A pair of power blue tailor made concealed pocket leather pants and matching underwear and shocks. And had his two-tone blue and white reptile shoes comfortably resting on the floor. A custom made white and blue trim tam was twisted backwards on his bald head, concealing most of it. While a modest flat-link 18kt gold chain choker hung loosely around his neck. He sat holding the steering wheel steady at twelve o'clock, very relaxed in the cream colored leather seat. Smiling enjoying the ride. Flashing an array of brilliant light from his half carat diamond watch and matching ring, with the slightest movement of his hand.

Francis had chosen her tailor made leather three-quarter length split-in-the-back grey skirt to wear. Tan sleeveless, pig's skin blouse. And pair of low-heel, two-tone loose leg fitting, grey and tan suede boots. A black silk turban was donning her head. And not to be out done by Slim, she had accented her neck with a black pearl necklace. And sat flashing her platinum half carat diamond watch and ring by inspecting her designer fingernails occasionally. The Rolls had "The Best of Earth, Wind, and Fire" bumping. Cruising on the highway doing a steady 55 mph.

They were on their way to rendezvous with Kathy and the kids. Because Epson was satisfied that David's confession had consequently solved the remaining cases. Since the evidence on file pointed to Alice and Janis killing Larry. And to themselves, after that, committing accidental suicide from a drug overdose. So for that reason Biggs had to immediately relinquish his company's hold on Kathy's 3 million dollar insurance settlement check. And the hold that was on the passports and visas that she had applied for, also had to be lifted.

As Kathy sat looking out of the window of the Boeing 747 at the clouds hovering around the snow cover peak of Mount Rainier she visualized the moment when Slim had said, "As soon as you walk out of that insurance company with the check, go pick up your travel papers and book a flight to Rio De Janeiro via Los Angeles. Then call and tell me what your scheduled arrival time will be in L.A., so Francis and I can meet you at the airport and pick up the kids. Then you'll fly on to Rio. Where Harry and Ginger will pick you up at the airport, and take you to the place they're going to stay with you until David gets out..." The reality of that and the Asians forgiving David's interest on his debt, plus, her share of Janis' porn film royalties made her utter, "Wow." As she continued to peer out the window port into the vassness of the sky her mind began to flash with sexual fantancies that forced her to cross her legs, squirm, then scurry to the ladies room. "I'll be right back," she told her kids. In there behind the privacy of the locked door she pulled down her slacks and panties to her ankles and cocked up her legs after she sat down and begn to finger her sopping wet slit imagining that she had nothing on but a thong and David had pulled it to one side to lick and suck between her legs. Then he made her get in position to be fucked in her tight pink colored virgin ass— not on a bed of roses, but one covered with nothing but hundred dollar bills. Gradually, she moaned louder and louder as she pressed her middle finger deeper and harder,until, her body stiffened, jerked, then relaxed in the estasy of cum streaming out of her pussy dripping into the comode. During that moment, she had been completely oblivious to the airline stewardess' inquiry, "Miss, are you alright in there?"

Chapter Seventeen
The Special News Report

Shortly after David's trial, NBS released a special news report about it that aired nationally on television.

"Good evening. Tonight we bring you a special report concerning the David Mitchell trial. As you may recall, he is the man who, two months ago, confessed to killing his thirteen year old retarded nephew but pled not guilty. What is now being alleged by city of Seattle police officials is that his wife, Kathy Mitchell, was the real killer. They believe David's confession to the murder of the boy was preplanned and later given to police as a decoy and ploy that would make it possible for his wife to collect three million dollars from her sister Janis Watson's life insurance policy then flee unimpeded with it to Brazil. A South American country beyond the reach of the long arm of the law here in the United States. For lack of an extradition treaty. However, the very first news reports about the case were focused on the tragic death of Larry Vargas. And tonight, NBS returns to that topic with this special report.

We begin this telecast by informing any viewers who missed our earlier coverage of the case, that it was rumored early on Larry Vargas was killed by members of the notorious Asian mafia gang in retaliation for a Diamond Security Guard Company employee's tip that led to an F.B.I. bust at the West Seattle based SeaLand commercial shipping company, just weeks before Vargas was brutally murdered at the La Villa Motel on

Rainier Avenue. Because the tip led to the arrest of many local members of the gang in connection with federal agent's confiscation of a large overseas shipment of illegal firearms, two hundred pounds of cocaine and heroin, plus, the deportation of about fifty Asian women that no doubt were destine to become prostitutes on the streets of Seattle.

We've returned our focus to the case again because Larry Vargas' mother Florantine has hired a private investigator name Alfred Martinez to help bring her son's killer to justice. Releasing a statement to the press saying, quote, "Whether, members of the Asian mafia. Or, two dead corpses." Referring to deceased– Alice Vargas and Janis Watson. Who, according to a diary police found belonging to Ms. Watson, were lesbian lovers who also planned to kill Larry for having sexual intercourse with Ms. Watson's retarded son. The same boy that David Mitchell confessed to murdering.

Martinez told our reporters that he wanted to separate fact from fiction. Get to the bottom of the truth. And did by concentrating on the evidence that appeared, at first glance to Seattle police detectives, to be insignificant. Questioning whether Alice Vargas and her close friend Janis Watson, verses, the Asian mafia had the best motive and opportunity to kill Larry? His conclusion was, not very likely the Asian mafia. Because, if not for injuring his back, Larry would have been at work on the evening he was murdered at the motel. So obviously the rumor that had been circulating he was killed by members of the local gang developed only because at the time of his murder he wore his Diamond Security Guard uniform.

What eliminated Larry's wife and her closest friend as his killers, was, Martinez discovering that a grand jury had refused to indict the two women on charges of first degree murder because the kitchen knives found in both women's purses tested negative for traces of blood. Only possible if they had never been used to kill Larry with. So he believed there had to be another explanation why his blood was found on the soles of their shoes and in the car of Janis Watson.

As he continued to prob it occurred to Martinez that whoever knew the answer to that question also knew who killed his client's beloved son. And it ironically turns out to be a woman who had come into an after hour hangout with credit cards belonging to Alice Vargas and Janis Watson, while David Mitchell was there gambling that night and overheard mention of the names on the cards. Janis was David's sister-in-law. Witnesses testified at David's trial that he and at least one other person walked out behind the woman and saw her leave in a cab. So Martinez checked with the Yellow Cab Company and traced the cab's record of destinations to the cab driver. And found out that he had picked the woman up that night at the home of Janis Watson then drove her to the Parkway Plaza Apartments and from there to the after hour spot and finally dropped her off on Union and 23rd Street.

After Martinez shared that information with the police department it was discovered that the address of the apartment building matched the address of a woman name Ruby Carson, who's currently on parole. When Carson was questioned, she told authorities a friend of hers name Tina Perez was the person who had come to her apartment. With jewelry she wanted to sell. And because Carson was wearing a piece of the jewelry when she was being questioned, police were able to prove that it belonged to Alice Vargas by matching the neckless with pictures they had of her wearing it.

Once Perez was in custody on charges of grand theft, possession of stolen credit cards, and facing the death penalty if convicted of first degree murder for intentionally injecting Alice Vargas and Janis Watson with a fatal dose of heroin in order to rob them, she agreed with Deputy Prosecutor Darrell Epson to provide him with the information that would lead to the arrest and conviction of the party responsible for murdering Larry Vargas. In exchange for her guilty plea to the solitary charge of involuntary manslaughter.

Perez explained, that, on the night Larry was murdered, earlier on in the evening, she had been working as a prostitute on Union and 23rd Street in the central district of Seattle to make enough money to buy narcotics and get high. After making enough she asked to be dropped off by her last customer at the La Villa Motel on Rainier. Where a dealer going by the street name Big Money was renting a room. And, according to Perez, is known to always come to town with the best street drugs that money can buy. While she lingered around on the backside of the motel waiting for Big Money's girlfriend to signal it was her turn to go in, she observed Larry Vargas and a man known as Low, because of his short height, go inside a motel room. Low's partner High, who's called that because of his tall height, came along a little bit afterwards and went into the same room, Perez said.

Police detectives then decided to reexamine the evidence that had been collected from Vargas' motel room and discovered marijuana cigarette butts. That discovery, along with the description Perez gave of the men, helped to create a 'heavy marijuana smokers' and 'partners in crime' profile on the men. Given that information, Washington State Department of Correction officials began to randomly question inmates, which, produced twelve potential candidates as suspects. Whose names and pictures were faxed to the detectives handling the case. Other individuals that were not candidates were then added to the montage and used by police to interview Perez with again. Authorities claim they did not disclose the height of any of the men in the pictures they asked her to look at. And she positively identified Otis Thompson, who is very short at five feet, and Cecil Hamilton, who's very tall at six feet two inches as High and Low. And last seen go into the motel room rented by Larry Vargas.

If you have any information concerning the whereabouts of these two men please contact Seattle police authorities immediately."

Another special report followed a week later. But this time the Fugitives On The Loose program aired it.

"...Ladies and gentlemen we are also happy to announce tonight that the two men Seattle, Washington police authorities wanted to apprehend in connection with the murder of Larry Vargas were captured today after attempting to rob a liquor store in Pittsburgh, Pennsylvania. Pittsburgh police say that Otis Thompson and Cecil Hamilton began a life on the run from Seattle authorities living as hobos. And reported that the men known as High and Low were in ragged dirty clothes, that stunk so bad, police dogs had to make the capture. Which we feel is befitting because they were acting like dogs when they slashed Larry Vargas' neck and stabbed him in the stomach, then left him to die in a puddle of his own blood..."

Chapter Eighteen
The Tragedy Of It All

Out of all the cases that Aaron McCalister had been involved with in his thirty years of police work it was the tragedy of the David Mitchell case that most intrigued him. And after he retired wrote a book about it. How the end game played out...

The fact that several marijuana butts had been found inside Larry's rented motel room meant that he had left the 8-Ball Tavern with Low going to purchase the grass with High knowing where to be at a designated spot and follow them at a safe distance back to the motel. All the while, Low was feeding Larry a lot of hype about how cool his friend was. That convinced Larry it was alright to let High in to smoke some of the weed with he and his partner when High knocked on the door claiming to be looking for Low. And at first, that was their only intentions. But what went dramatically wrong was Larry had been heavily drinking because of the situation that he was caught in by his wife and Ken's mother and was half drunk when he started smoking the marijuana. Which gave him the hallucination that it was OK to tell his new friends about it. But it wasn't alright to talk about it because he was in the company of two scandalous individuals who had been to prison, and like most of the hard core bunch there, they hated rapist and child molesters. And became infuriated to unwittingly find themselves socializing with one getting high. So they collaborated and tricked Larry into a position where High could grab him from behind and muffle his mouth while Low stabbed him in the stomach and slashed his neck. Then grabbed the rest of the marijuana that hadn't been smoked and got out of the room in a hurry leaving Larry for dead. But he managed to drag himself as far as to the front of the motel trying to get help then collapsed in the parking lot and bled to death.

Next. After Alice and Janis went there looking for Larry Tina showed up there herself to buy narcotics from Big Money. Then after she got the drugs left the motel room looking for customers and spotted Alice and Janis sitting in Janis' car in front of the motel in the parking lot and talked her way into the backseat. Shortly afterwards, Larry staggered out of the motel room he'd rented on the backside of the building and collapsed in plain sight of Alice and Janis. They both got out to take a closer look. But Tina, knowing that she needed a ride to get away from there and didn't want to lose her potential sale, stayed in the car. Alice and Janis went too close and unknowingly made the mistake of accidently stepping into Larry's blood. Then panicked when they recognized him. And drove off with the knives they had in their purses and with Tina in the backseat with her drugs. During the ride Tina convinced them that 'at a moment like this' she had exactly what they needed. And all it took was that first hit on her crack pipe and Alice and Janis were hooked. And consumed more coke than they could handle. Then when they complained to Tina that they needed to come down the only thing she had that could do it was the heroin she had. Being the dope fiend that she was she always carried extra syringes with her. Not a problem ever since the aids prevention campaign got started and needles, just like condoms, were given away free. What was a problem, until she figured out a way to solve it, was getting a needle into the arm of both women and simultaneously injecting them so they'd pass out at the same time. "Look. All I have is some heroin if you want me to give you something to bring you down. And probably, in case this ever happens again, you need to know how to do what you gotta do for yourself. So, I'm gonna show you." First she pulled out the kit she had tucked in her panties with the dope, syringes, cooker, cotton, spoon, butane lighter, and tie in it. And told Janis and Alice they needed to find something to tie off their arms with too. So they did. And brung Tina the half full glass of water that she requested. She showed them how to cook and draw it up. Then they watched her put the needle to her arm and tap it into a vein while holding the tie in her mouth, and saw a swirl of blood invade the light brown liquid in the narrow tube when the tip of the needle pierced the vein. "After that, then you loosen up the tie," she explained. Tina repositioned the tie after that so that it held the syringe in place stuck in her arm. Then she helped both women get to that point themselves. "OK. Now is when you press the plunger down and run it in like this," she said and demonstrated at the same time. She told the prosecuting attorney, that, when she realized how potent the stuff was it was too late to stop Janis and Alice from running it in and dying on her.

Finally. It was very misfortunate for young Kenny Watson that his uncle David happened to be at the gambling house and overheard who the credit cards belonged to that Tina managed to peddle off. And was prompted by that to leave his poker game and go to his sister-in-law's house, only to find her and her best friend there dead. After he had, obviously his first instinct was to call Slim Shaky, his millionaire stepfather, and tell his mother. After he did, then tragically, the three of them could do nothing but helplessly listen to the sorid cries and scuffling sounds penetrate their ears creating a horrible picture of the ghastly event taking place on the other end of the line. Kathy cursing and blaming her nephew as she awoke and drug him out of bed into the bathroom. Where she and his cousins whom he had loved so much each did their part in helping each other to kill him. He never had a chance against them. Poor Ken. Poor Ding Ding.

THE END

Printed in the United States
138529LV00006B/108/P